BETTER THE DEVIL YOU KNOW

BEY DECKARD

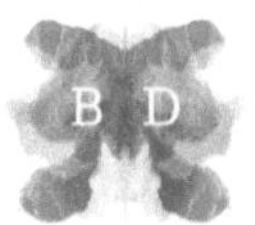

ISBN: 978-1-989250-21-1

CONTENTS

Soundtrack

https://geni.us/DevilOST

Author's Note & Content Warnings

I'm going to make you read the warnings, even if you've read them before, so what follows doesn't take anyone by surprise.

This horror novel contains:
Graphic torture, forced incest, and rape
This is a work of *fiction*. If you're ok with all that… carry on.

†

Thanks to Starr Waddell for the amazing editing job and to Varian Krylov for the gorgeous pic for the cover. Thank you to Sarabeth Miller and Joseph Lance Tonlet for beta reading for me.
I'm dedicating this book to the folks out there that love a good psycho.

"Stand back, Tom Devil, Lord, I'm gonna rule hell by myself."

— *STAGGOLEE* BY PACIFIC GAS & ELECTRIC

THE MONSTER

Byron slowly pulled apart the loose knot in the sash, then let the robe fall from his shoulders. It gave him a frisson as it slid, cool and soft, down his back. With a smile, he gathered up the slippery, blood-red material and draped it over the back of the Queen Anne chair that sat just inside the entrance to his sanctuary.

Drawing out the anticipation, he purposefully kept his gaze away from the dais as he crossed to the other side of the room. A teak panel opened in the wall at a touch, and he pressed one of the buttons within. A moment later, Broschi's "Ombra Fedele Anch'io" stroked the air almost tentatively with its opening notes. Byron filled his lungs and closed his eyes, letting the music infuse him with the quiet joy it always brought. When the male soprano's supple voice began to rise above the strings, Byron breathed out slowly and finally turned his attention to what awaited him in the centre of the rotunda.

The young man's eyes were wide and wet, his pupils huge with the cocktail of drugs coursing through his veins. He let out a strangled, animalistic moan as Byron climbed the stairs naked, his cock primed and bobbing stiffly as he neared.

His victim was pretty… so very pretty—blond and pale, with smooth skin and beautifully rounded, pert buttocks for someone so thin. He reached out and stroked the hollow of the young man's cheek, gazing down at him benevolently like a priest about to give the Sacrament. As his thumb brushed the sutures where he had sewn just the corners of the young man's mouth shut, he smiled. Byron had made him even more pretty when he had turned him into the perfect vessel.

The boy made another gurgling sound at the touch, and more red-tinged saliva ran down his chin. Toothless and with his bloodied jaw propped open by small nails embedded in the pits where his molars once sat, he knelt, ready to receive Byron. Not that he had a choice *but* to kneel—the hooks set into the flesh beneath his thin clavicles were attached to chains that hung from the ceiling, supporting him in the position. However, the way he listed slightly and the tearing around one of the metal hooks suggested that perhaps one of his bones had finally given under his weight. It was no matter. Byron was nearly done with him anyway.

With a warm smile, he grasped the boy's head in his hands and brought his cock into contact with the perfect-sized hole he had made of his mouth. Slowly, almost gently, he pushed his swollen glans past the constricting *O* of the young man's sewn lips and then timed his first hard thrust with the rising crescendo of the singer's rich voice as it echoed in the round chamber. He sunk his cock deep into his victim's throat, crushing his face to his pelvis; the young man convulsed against him, his throat muscles tightening around his shaft as his body fought to expel him. Finally, he pulled all the way back, and his cock popped from the young man's ravaged mouth, slimed in blood and fluids.

"Glorious," he whispered. "You are glorious."

The young man's breathing had a slushy quality to it as he struggled to take in air, and it was obvious that he wouldn't last much longer. He was barely holding on to consciousness, and

Byron knew that no amount of drugs could continue to prolong his usefulness. He'd been his vessel for nearly a week now.

"You should be proud," he murmured as he fed his cock into the bloody, torn mouth once more. "You're doing so well…"

The boy's eyes bulged, and though Byron couldn't hear anything over the music, he could feel the vibrations of his muffled sob before the thick cockhead plugging his throat cut it off. However, before Byron could get into a good rhythm, a spasm shook the young man, and his eyes rolled up in his head. Cursing, Byron pulled his dick out of his victim's mouth and watched him twitch hard, the hook in his broken shoulder dragging further through flesh as he sagged and let out one last rattling breath.

Byron sighed. So frustrating.

Why couldn't he have lasted just a minute longer?

For a moment Byron only stared at the dead body hanging limp in his chains, the young man's face slack and eyes unseeing. He was useless to him now, of course; Byron wasn't some sick pervert who liked to have sex with corpses. With a headshake, he closed the drip of the IV that fed into the young man's neck, and stretching his expression into a bright smile, he turned to the figure strapped to the metal chair.

Slow tears leaked down the man's face as he stared at his son's body, but no sound came from him save for a breathy hiss that escaped his gaping mouth. The cut across his throat was healing nicely under the neat sutures, but the same couldn't be said about the myriad other incisions spaced along his chest; most of them were inflamed, and despite the antibiotics, there was only a pitiful amount of dark urine in the bag at the man's feet. Byron knew that his kidneys were shutting down as he succumbed to sepsis.

Byron pulled on the catheter that trailed from the bandaged cauterized wound in the man's crotch. As the bloody tubing slid free, the man shuddered in his bonds, and had Byron not severed his vocal chords, the hitched gasp would have undoubtedly been a cry. Something occurred to Byron then, and he frowned, glancing back at the corpse. Hollowing out parts of the man's severed penis and filling it with Plaster of Paris to harden it into a dildo had been a *wonderful* idea at the time. Having the man watch his own disembodied cock plunder his son's virgin ass had been worth the effort alone. But, when Byron had lost his grip on the slippery thing and it penetrated further into the young man's body, out of reach, he hadn't really thought much about the consequences. Play had brought him to a heightened pinnacle of arousal, and messy little details like that tended to fall by the wayside. Thinking about it now, he realized that having a rotting penis lodged in his rectum hadn't helped prolong the young man's life any. He made a mental note to attach some sort of cord to the severed member, should he try such a thing again.

Humming along to the next track on his *Lustrations* playlist—Cassidy's "Vide Cor Meum"—he unrolled his leather medical kit and slid his favourite scalpel out, placing it on the stained ivory surface of the antique pedestal. The man strapped to the chair shook his head as vigorously as his weak state allowed him, and Byron laid a kind hand on his shoulder.

"It will all be over soon. But you have one last thing to do for me since your son couldn't perform," he said gently. He reached for the small bottle containing the potent mix he had designed to keep his victims alert but also shield them somewhat from the effects of shock—benzo, lidocaine, DMT being the main components—and measured out a large dose in the antique glass syringe. Almost as soon as he had injected the drugs into the man's venous catheter, his victim's face slackened and his movements became even more sluggish. Head hanging to the side, breath whistling past lips gone bloodless, the man barely twitched as Byron slid the scalpel's blade through skin and muscle, into his diaphragm.

Byron's erection had begun to flag, but when the man's thin blood began flowing down his chest, his dick stiffened to rock at the anticipation.

The previous times he had used the man's body like this, he had simply severed skin from muscle and used the tight pockets he created in the man's flesh to bring himself to climax. Afterwards, he had simply sewn the offerings he'd left behind into the skin. This time was different… He wanted to feel the beat of his heart against his cock.

Carefully, he cut into the man's body, thrusting his fingers deep into the hole he made in the pleura; by attempting to free up space in the thoracic cavity, he effectively cut the left lung away. Blood bubbles popped and spattered Byron's chest as he worked as quickly as he could to make the man ready to receive him. He didn't have much time left.

Byron grabbed a second syringe and sent a milligram of atropine directly into the man's jugular. The man's head lifted instantly. He hissed out a thick-sounding breath, the tendons rigid in his neck as Byron straddled his thighs. Then he slumped backwards, a bloody foam on his lips, and Byron pushed his cock up into the incision beneath his sternum. With a grunt, he thrust hard and felt tissues part and the edge of rib slide against the top of his shaft. He wrapped his arms around the man's head, holding him to his breast as gently as a lover as he fucked his body cavity for a few short plunges before he went deep. And then… There it was… The heart had gone tachy with the shot, and it vibrated against his cockhead.

"Yes!" Byron pressed his face to the top of the man's head, just holding himself in place while the dying heart danced against his cock. The man's one good lung swelled with his irregular, rapid breathing and squeezed and caressed him. Tears trickled from the corners of Byron's eyes as he crushed them shut, transported with ecstasy as the soprano's note held in Mozart's "Der Hölle Rache," the sound pure and beautiful. With a cry, he finally climaxed, bathing the heart with semen as it slowed.

By the time he had finished, the heart had stilled and the aria had ended. Only his own panting breaths marred the silence for a moment before the gentle strings of Handel's "Cara Sposa" crept quietly into the space.

With a wince, Byron climbed off the dead man's lap, his cock a gory, dripping mess. He lifted his eyes to the stars visible beyond the glass dome above his workspace and raised his arms, bloodied nearly to the elbow, and silently thanked whatever forces there were for the desires that drove him. He was a god among men; it was a heady gift indeed.

Behind him, the door opened quietly, and he heard the click of Gloria's heels on the travertine. He smiled and turned around. Dressed in an exquisitely tailored slate-grey Alexander McQueen suit, she stood tall and elegant at the foot of the stairs. Gloria's dark eyes took in the mess atop the dais, and she arched a shapely eyebrow at him.

"You're done, I imagine?" she asked in her velvet-smooth voice. She stepped gracefully to the side to avoid the rivulet of blood that was inching its way towards her Louboutins.

Byron laughed and nodded. He descended the stairs and twisted the knob in the small open shower space set into the wall. He tested the water before stepping into it and watched diluted blood swirl down the drain set into the floor.

"Shall I have the cleaners come tonight, or would you rather tomorrow?" asked Gloria, coming closer. She held her tablet against her forearm, finger held above its surface.

Soaping himself quickly, Byron pondered for a moment. He disliked having strangers around while he was at home, but he had no plans for the evening.

Gloria noted his hesitation and spoke up.

"I think I may have found something promising for you," she said with a smile. "That is, if you're not too tired to go out."

Byron frowned. Tired, no—sated... yes. But that wasn't a bad thing when it came to new quarry. It just meant he was more likely to draw things out.

"No, I'm fine," he replied after a moment. "What did you have in mind?"

"You've made a new friend on one of your accounts. I've been messaging with them, and it seems like a good match. It's a man… Is that all right?" she asked, looking up from her tablet.

Nodding impatiently, Byron finished rinsing himself and turned the water off. Gloria handed him a towel as he stepped out of the shower.

"He's young, attractive, has no family to speak of… Hmm, let's see. He has good taste in music, restaurants… Oh, and I took the liberty of making reservations at *Le Clin d'Oeil* for tonight in case he piqued your interest."

Byron glanced at her. Part of him was irritated that she would just assume he'd want to go, but knowing Gloria, she already had a contingency plan should he turn down the suggestion. He smiled.

"Yes… Why not? What time?"

"Eight fifteen. I reserved your favourite table."

It didn't give him a lot of time to get ready, but he nodded again. He dropped the towel on the floor and accepted the robe from Gloria.

"Sounds good. Have the car brought around at seven, and make sure that the cleaners arrive only after I've gone. Oh, and I wasn't happy about the way they moved everything around last time. I want to come back to a pristine room with everything in its proper place."

"Yes, sir," Gloria said, typing on her tablet. "I'll see to it myself."

"Good." With the silk of the robe sticking to his back where he was still wet, he tied the sash and walked across the cool floor to stop the music, cutting off Caballe's soaring soprano mid-aria. Keeping in step, Gloria followed him down the richly carpeted hallway to the grand staircase where she stopped at its base. As he climbed the stairs, she called up to him.

"The Richardsons were satisfactory, then?"

Byron paused on the step, hand on the mahogany railing, and

thought back to the moving heat of the man's heart against his flesh. He chuckled low with a nod.

"Yes, Gloria. They were quite satisfactory. You did well." He glanced over his shoulder at his assistant. A subtle smile curled Gloria's full lips before she turned away, fingers flying over the tablet's keyboard as she got things ready for his date.

THE MAN

Byron's favourite table was in the very back corner of the restaurant against the big windows overlooking the bay. It commanded a spectacular view of the city, and he often came here on his own to watch the boats sail in and out of the harbour whilst he ate his duck pâté and herb-crusted calf liver. Though he was almost twenty minutes early, the traffic on the bridge having been light, the man he was meeting was already there. He was seated with his back to the room and seemed to be lost in thought as he looked out over the water. Gloria had shown Bryon a few encouraging pictures, but the young man was even more compelling in person. He had dark hair, kept a little longer on the top than what Byron normally liked, and he was bearded, which was a change from all the clean-shaven men Gloria tended to pair him with.

However, his profile was attractive with a high forehead, straight nose, and lips that had an interesting fullness to them. When he noticed Byron's approach and turned, his eyes widened, and Byron guessed that they would be a warm chocolate-brown in the sun—they were beautiful eyes. Kind, trusting eyes. A bright smile lit up the young man's face, and he quickly stood.

"Hello! And here I thought I would have more time to get over my nerves," said the young man with a self-conscious laugh.

With a smile, Byron looked over his shoulder.

"I could leave and come back, if you'd like?" he said in a light tone.

The man laughed again, a rich sound against the quiet classical music coming from the speakers overhead.

"No. That's ok. I think I'll be fine," he replied. "Michael." He held out his hand, and Byron tilted his head. None of this awkward hug or kiss-kiss business that a lot of men and women normally imposed on him. He gratefully accepted the handshake.

"Byron. A pleasure," he said, his smile widening, and gestured to the table. "Sit, please."

As soon as they had taken their seats, Angélique arrived at the table in her starched white shirt and black slacks.

"Bonsoir, Monsieur Smith," she said. With her accent, the fake name he liked to use came out as "Smeet," and it never failed to bring a smile to his face.

"Bonsoir, Angélique. Le *Château Pradeaux 2008*, s'il vous plaît… avec"—he turned to Michael, and the young man nodded quickly—"deux verres. Merci."

"Je vous en prie," murmured the blond woman, and she left them to find the red wine he so enjoyed.

"You know French?" asked Byron, surprised.

Michael grinned a little shyly and looked down for a moment, his dark hair falling into his eyes. He brushed it back and nodded, meeting Byron's gaze again.

"Yeah. I've picked some up over the years… here and there." There was something incredibly charming about the way he licked his lips a little nervously before giving him another demure smile.

Byron thought Michael looked oddly familiar, but he couldn't bring to mind where he could have seen him before. The height of his cheekbones, the slant of his eyebrows, the way the tip of his nose moved subtly as he talked… It was like a memory…

His thoughts were interrupted when Angélique reappeared with the wine and two glasses, and he and Michael sat in silence, watching her open the bottle. After depositing the cork carefully on the table, she held the wine up, the question evident on her face. Byron gestured to Michael, and Angélique poured a small amount of wine into his glass. Michael picked it up but didn't immediately put it to his lips like Byron expected him to. Instead, he swirled it twice in the glass and then held it beneath his nose. When he seemed satisfied, he took a tiny sip. His eyes widened.

"Wow. This is really good," he said, looking up at Angélique. The woman smiled and ducked her head in a pleased nod before pouring a measure in each of their glasses. After she had recited the day's specials and taken their orders—*Le Clin d'Oeil* didn't believe in printed menus—Michael shook his head at Byron.

"Are you trying to impress me with what I figure's going to be an *outrageously* expensive meal? Because… I'm impressed. My wallet, not so much, but… this"—he held up the glass of wine—"is amazing."

Byron held up his own glass and brought it close to Michael's.

"To first… and lasting impressions," he said. Michael laughed and repeated the toast before touching his glass to Byron's.

DESPITE THE FACT THAT HE WAS ONLY THERE TO LURE Michael back to his abode—should he be suitable—and set him up in the converted atrium he used as his workspace sanctuary, Byron found himself thoroughly caught up in the conversation. Michael, although he claimed a strictly blue-collar background, peppered his speech with phrases in Italian, French, and German, among others. Byron liked the way he gestured enthusiastically as he talked and traced out shapes on the white tablecloth with a fingertip to illustrate his points. Michael was intelligent without being arrogant and optimistic without seeming overly naïve. The longer they spoke, the more Byron became… unsure of himself.

Byron frowned at his crème brûlée. The problem was that he was honestly enjoying himself just talking to Michael. He couldn't remember the last time he had felt a similar connection with another human being, and it was confusing him. He glanced up and saw Michael was watching him, his dark eyes curious. For a moment, Byron thought about simply paying the check, kissing the young man on the cheek, and walking out of his life. He smiled at Michael and let out a silent sigh at the shy attraction he saw soften the young man's face in return—he was so beautiful and selflessly charming. Maybe it was the earlier play session with the Richardsons that had put Byron in this mellow, forgiving mood. Yes, maybe he would spare him…

Michael reached across the table and put his hand on top of Byron's.

The contact made Byron's heart kick up in excitement, and for the first time, he saw something a little darker in Michael's eyes.

"I hope you're not thinking of calling it an early night," said the young man softly. "I thought we might, you know, go somewhere more private?" His thumb slid under Byron's palm, and Byron stared down at their hands. "I want to get to know you better."

No, you don't…

If he brought Michael home, Michael wouldn't survive the encounter. The moment stretched out, and when Byron glanced back up, Michael licked his lips and frowned. He began to pull away, made unsure by the long silence, but Byron's hand turned of its own volition and captured Michael's in a soft hold.

"Yes. Yes, that sounds like a good idea," he said, making a decision. "Your place or mine?" It was such clichéd line, but the answer would decide Michael's fate. Byron thought he saw something in Michael's face that gave him pause—something shrewd—but it was gone in an instant, replaced by another endearingly shy smile. Byron pushed his glass of whiskey away; sometimes drink made him paranoid.

"Yours—if that's ok? I have a feeling you have the nicer place," said Michael with a quiet laugh.

Well… that's that *then*, Byron thought.

With a wide grin at Michael, he nodded and squeezed his hand before signalling to Angélique for the check.

Byron groaned softly as Michael licked the head of his cock with a soft, flat tongue, teasing him. His other hand was cupping Byron's testicles and squeezing them in a way that made him squirm and wish he could rid himself of his pants entirely. The backseat of the Audi A8 was roomy, but it was still awkward, and despite his driver's discretion, the man's presence was a little distracting. Thankfully, the road was clear of its usual spring fog, and they were soon pulling into the huge circular driveway that fronted his property. After they'd tugged their clothes somewhat back into place, Byron helped Michael out of the car and chuckled at his expression when he gaped up at the house.

"*This* is where you live?"

Byron looked up fondly at the turn-of-the-century manor with its big windows and neoclassical façade.

"Yes. I inherited it when my parents passed about ten years ago."

"Oh, I'm sorry," said Michael, and he placed a hand on Byron's lower back. Strangely rattled by the unexpected heat that rose inside him at the gentle touch, Byron thought again about sending Michael home alone to the little apartment in the Heights he had mentioned. He might be disappointed or even angry with the outcome of the evening, but he would be safe… safe from the terrible, *beautiful* things that Byron would be unable to keep himself from doing once they were through those doors.

However, before he could speak, Michael climbed the stairs and closed the window of opportunity. With a grim smile, Byron followed him up the steps and punched in his code. Michael opened the door and let out a low whistle as he entered.

"Holy shit. Jesus *fucking* Christ… oh sorry"—he glanced over at Byron, his cheeks dimpled—"sometimes I can't control my mouth, but this is some pad you've got here, mister." He trailed his fingers over the top of the carved rosewood table that sat in the middle of the entrance and stared in amazement at the walls with their heavy, dark mouldings and huge oil paintings. His eyes went to the grand staircase, and he craned his head back with a grin. "Shall we?"

Byron smiled indulgently but shook his head. No, the bedroom was not for Michael.

"I thought we would have another drink first… I have a particularly fine artisanal bourbon I think you might like."

Obvious disappointment flashed across Michael's face.

"Ok… I guess that sounds good," he said, his tone begrudging. However, his wide-eyed enthusiasm returned when he took in the sumptuously appointed living room with its thick carpeting, soft, black leather couches, and marble fireplace. He crossed the room and sank into one of the sofas with a contented sigh.

Byron walked to the bar in the corner and set about pouring drinks for the two of them. With his back to the room, he mixed some Ketamine into one of the vintage lowball glasses.

"So you live here all by yourself?"

Nodding, Byron crossed the room and handed the drugged bourbon to Michael. Michael touched the rim of his glass to Byron's and took a small sip as his host settled down next to him on the couch.

"Doesn't it get lonely?" Michael's brown eyes were shadowed by lashes that were long and dark—when he looked up searchingly at Byron, the older man felt something that was very nearly pity. He took a mouthful of his own bourbon, savouring it for a moment. The drug would take full effect in a few minutes; he had time to kill.

"Yes. Sometimes, it is a little lonely," he replied in all honesty after he'd swallowed. However, the loneliness was just a small price to pay for what the privacy allowed him.

Michael moved a little closer to him, his face flushed.

"Well, I'm here now…" It was an invitation to kiss those soft lips again, but Byron didn't dare. Instead, he lifted a hand and threaded his fingers through the hair at the back of Michael's head, massaging his scalp gently with his fingertips.

"Mmm…" Michael brought the glass to his lips again and swallowed down the rest of the bourbon before closing his eyes and leaning into the touch. "That feels really good."

Byron curled his fingers and tugged on Michael's hair, eliciting a small pleased sigh from the young man. Then he deposited his glass on the marble coffee table and plucked the empty one from Michael's hand before it fell to the floor. Michael's eyes fluttered open drowsily.

"I really like you," Michael whispered and stroked his hand up Byron's thigh. It seemed like the drug had taken hold.

"I don't often say this," replied Byron with his brows knit, "but I like you too." He'd take his time with Michael… Make him last. Be careful and slow. Michael's dark hair was soft and silken, and he ran his fingers through it again, marvelling at the feeling of it against his skin. Michael stared up at him, his beautiful face made smooth by his vague, sleepy expression.

Byron found his eyes drawn to the licked wetness of Michael's bottom lip, the way it caught the light as he breathed. Plump bottom lip… healthy and pink—Byron would sink his teeth into it. Shaking his head, he blinked a few times to rid himself of a little light-headedness and then leaned forward to press his mouth to the side of Michael's neck.

Smooth, warm skin… a hint of cologne. He breathed in deep.

"Yes, perfect," he murmured and then frowned in confusion when he realized his hand was no longer stroking Michael's hair. It took a bit of effort to open his eyes, and he looked blearily around.

"What's… happening?" Everything looked slightly out of focus, and it took immense concentration just to sit up. His body felt heavy… strange.

Michael let out a low chuckle, his eyes bright and alert as he stared down at Byron slumped over on the sofa. Bewildered, Byron watched as his grinning guest lifted one of his nerveless hands to his lips to bestow a mischievous kiss on his knuckles.

"Drugged… me?" Byron mumbled through numb lips. "How?"

"Ah, just a simple trick, my dear sir," replied Michael with a smirk, all traces of meekness wiped from his face. He dropped Byron's hand in his lap and reached over him to grab Byron's glass from the table. There was still a finger of the golden liquid inside, and Michael lifted it to his lips. Frozen in his husk of a body, Byron watched him drink it down—though all his senses felt muffled, his brain sped along a terrible, confused path. Fear began to take hold.

"Whu…" he tried, but couldn't make his tongue or lips form the words. His saliva felt thick in his throat, and he attempted to swallow but failed. A strangled moan came from his open mouth.

Michael licked his lips and looked at the empty lowball glass.

"You were right. That was very fine indeed," he said and then tossed the glass at the fireplace where it shattered on the marble. "But I've had better."

He stood and rubbed his hands together.

"Now… Why don't you show me where you do your best work? I've been *dying* to see it with my own eyes," he said and laughed at his choice of words. He gestured with one hand. "Shall we, *Herr Unmensch*?"

As if Byron were being lifted by invisible hands, he rose to his feet, head lolling and limbs slack. When Michael began to hum softly, Byron could only watch as he was marched forward like a puppet on strings, leading his guest directly to the house's hallowed inner sanctum.

Role Reversal

Byron had vague recollections of being stripped naked… of being strapped down to the cold metal tilt table… of music he didn't recognize… of hands touching him… strangely gentle…

Groggy, he slowly lifted his head and looked around. Rock music played from the speakers set into the walls all around him. To his left, Michael stood in front of the big cupboard where Byron kept his tools and toys. He had one of the flat, velvet-lined drawers pulled out and was peering down at what was displayed there.

"Fffff…" Byron tried, but the drug still had his tongue pinned down. Michael's head came up at the sound, and he spun on his heel with a bright smile.

"What was that?" he asked, his head cocked.

"Shhhffff…" It was impossible. How had Michael switched the glasses? Then Byron remembered the way he had drunk from both tumblers, and the panic that had mellowed to a soft pulse in his gut reared up cold and fierce. "Hhhuuuhhh."

"I'm sorry, but I can't understand a word," laughed Michael, an impish glint in his eyes. "Shall I help?" He lifted a hand and snapped his fingers.

Instantly, Byron's head cleared. He blinked, too stunned to react for a moment. He had to have been injected with something… but what? He glanced around but saw no IV line, and Michael was halfway across the room. With a grunt, he strained up against his bonds, but he knew it was useless. No one had ever escaped from this table before—why should he fare differently? Byron ground his teeth together and forced himself to *think*.

"Feeling better?" asked Michael.

Byron remained silent, but the young man just shrugged and turned back to the cupboard. When the table Byron was tied to began to tilt up on its own to put him upright, he closed his eyes. It had to be the Ketamine causing hallucinations—that was the only explanation for how these things were happening to him. Only barely satisfied with that answer, he locked away the useless fear churning in the pit of his stomach and looked over at Michael. He watched him pick through a few items before he lifted one with a low whistle of appreciation.

"I haven't seen one of these in *ages*," he said, turning the key at the top of the anal pear to open it up. Michael looked over at Byron. "Wow—this isn't a reproduction, is it? Where in the world did you find this?"

"On eBay," Byron replied quietly. It had cost him a small fortune.

Michael let out a surprised laugh.

"Of course on eBay. Lord, is there anything you can't get on there, I wonder." He deposited the medieval torture device back in its place on the plush black velvet. "And this?" he asked, holding up an antique bone saw with an ivory handle. "eBay too?"

Byron shook his head.

"Estate sale." It was pure agony watching this complete stranger touching his belongings—this man… this *boy* who had somehow turned the tables on him and trapped him in his own web. He would watch, be patient, wait for Michael to make a mistake, and then he would have him. But how to get free?

"Estate sale," Michael repeated thoughtfully with a little nod. "Amazing what you can get at those."

"Who are you?" asked Byron, his eyes locked on Michael's hands as he rifled through another drawer. "What do you want from me?"

Ignoring the questions, his guest lifted out the phallic blade harness. With brows furrowed, he held it aloft by its leather straps and stared at it, obviously confused by what he was seeing. His face smoothed out in recognition a moment later.

"Holy shit! This is from that movie… fuck… the one with Brad Pitt and that guy from *The Usual Suspects*, isn't it?" he said, sounding excited. He glanced at Byron for confirmation.

"*Se7en.*"

"What kind of sick nutjob made it for you?"

Byron just stared at him, his mind caught up in escape… in retaliation.

Gloria should be around soon enough.

As if his thoughts had conjured her into being, his stately assistant stepped through the door holding the SIG P220 from the hidden case just outside the entrance to the rotunda. She had it at arm's length in a rigid Isosceles stance, the pistol steady in her long-fingered hands as she trained it on Michael.

"Not a moment too soon," he said lightly. Michael's head swivelled at his words, and he fixed Byron with brows knit.

Gloria's nostrils flared slightly, her jaw tight for a moment as she watched her target.

"Kill or cripple, sir?"

Byron laughed low. Death would not come for a long time to this foolish, foolish boy who thought he could take down one such as himself.

"I don't want him too damaged, my dear."

"Who do you think you're talking to?" asked Michael. He put down the harness, wiped his hands on his chinos, and climbed the three steps back to where Byron stood in his restraints, strapped to the table. The muzzle of the big gun followed his movements.

"You're no one," answered Byron with a sneer.

Michael shook his head like he couldn't believe what he was hearing.

"No. I'm serious. *Who* are you talking to? Who do you see?" He looked over his shoulder at Gloria standing still as stone at the entrance to the room. A small, confident smile curled her lip as she decided where to put the bullet.

Confused by Michael's question, Byron scowled.

"Don't bother with the head games. It's not going to work. Gloria will shoot you, and then you will get to see my work first-hand."

"Gloria?" asked Michael. "Your supposed personal assistant?" He turned back and stared hard at Byron for a moment. "There is no Gloria." His gaze flicked from one of his captive's eyes to the other, as if trying to read him.

Byron scoffed at Michael's ridiculous pronouncement.

"What are you talking about?"

Michael's brows went high.

"There *is* no Gloria," he repeated. "Come on. There's no one here but us."

Byron blinked rapidly a few times, and Michael's hand came up to stroke his cheek softly. There was a curious look on his face. Byron shifted away from the touch as best as he could.

"I have no idea what you're talking about. Gloria's been working for me for years."

Michael just chuckled with a small headshake.

"You really believe that, don't you?"

Doubt began to filter in, and Byron looked over at his assistant. She stared at him, her eyes large and dark.

Gloria... tall, almost regal in bearing. Always dressed impeccably. Efficient. Incredibly discreet.

"Yes, doesn't she seem too good to be true? Tell me... How did you meet her?" asked Michael, stepping back. Byron furrowed his brow. "What was the interview process like? How did you find her? Is there some kind of newspaper for your kind where you can place an ad: 'Serial Killer Looking For PA. Good Dental and Benefits'?"

Byron opened his mouth but, confused, found that he couldn't reply. How had Gloria come into his employ?

"Who is she, Byron?" asked Michael, leaning closer. His breath was warm against the side of Byron's face, his voice intimate.

Gloria. Who is Gloria?

"I… don't know," he replied after a moment. Maybe he was in a dream. Maybe he was still unconscious from the dose of Ketamine. Ingested, it could take hours to wear off.

"I'll tell you a story then, shall I?" Michael grabbed the metal chair with the shackles and dragged it over. He sat down in it and crossed one leg over the other. "Once upon a time…"

Gordon Jerome Samuels – 1966–1985

Gloria tried to keep from tugging down on the microskirt she was wearing as she paced back and forth along the little piece of sidewalk that she rented six days a week from the Gideon sisters. Even though it was only the start of her shift, her feet were already killing her. However, standing still wasn't really any better. The thin bomber jacket she wore open over her tiny tube top was doing little to keep her warm. At least when she was pacing, she wasn't as cold. It was a damn slow night.

She pulled the soft pack of Virginia Slims out of her knock-off Chanel purse and peered inside it. Only two smokes left. Gloria chewed on the corner of her lip, the taste of her cheap lipstick waxy and perfumed, and put the pack back into her bag with a sigh.

If she managed to get four transactions tonight, she would buy herself another pack to celebrate. And maybe one of those cheap bottles of sweet wine she liked. Gloria smiled to herself and spun in her towering heels to stalk back along the sidewalk. "Transactions" sounded so much better than "tricks" in her mind. And that's what they were, really. She shared her body for an amount of time in return for money; it was a business transaction… nothing more.

A blast of heated air warmed her momentarily as a man left the rundown motel she had stopped in front of—head down and hands in his pockets, he looked guilty. Gloria shook her head and watched him turn the corner.

Men. She honestly didn't know why so many of them seemed so ashamed of paying for sex. There wasn't anything *wrong* with it. It was no different than paying for a therapist or having a good massage. Besides, a lot of the girls, especially on this end of the block, could offer men something they couldn't get back home.

Ain't nothing wrong with that, she thought with a small nod. Plus, these men would pay for her legal name change and the surgery that would rid her of the last bit of the boy called Gordon she had once been. Everyone would be happy. The downside, of course, was that she would no longer appeal to these types of johns afterwards, but she figured after her recovery she could find something better. Like maybe a job working at an animal shelter— something *normal*. For now though, she was able to command a good price because of what was between her legs, and that was good. She was also a lot prettier than the other girls… Or at least that's what people kept telling her.

After another trip down the sidewalk, Gloria spotted a car driving slowly down the street. The headlights were spaced far apart, but it was low to the ground—a big boat of a car that crawled towards her, headlights bobbing from the uneven pavement. She let the jacket fall from her shoulders and thrust out her chest to show off the tiny but perfect tits that the hormones she couldn't really afford had granted her. Putting a little extra-saucy hip-swing into her strut, she approached the car.

A temporary situation for a permanent solution… a temporary situation for a permanent solution… She recited her mantra in her head as she licked her lips to make them shine in the light cast by the streetlight above her. *This guy* has *to stop. Why else would he be driving so slowly? He has to be looking for something. Please please please…*

Gloria smiled as the car pulled up right beside her. The driver's side window was down, and behind the wheel was a man with blond hair that was cut short and styled with a part to one side, giving him a bit of an old-fashioned look, though he couldn't be much older than she was. He was clean-shaven, tanned, had nicely shaped lips and a little cleft in his chin. When he smiled, he showed off even, white teeth. Gloria saw that he was wearing expensive-looking preppy clothes: a white V-neck sweater over a light-grey button-down. He was gorgeous… Though if she really had to be nitpicky and find fault with him, his eyes were a little strange. They were an icy-pale, flat blue. She leaned against the car door and tried to ignore the fact that he didn't seem to have blinked once since stopping.

A dead man's eyes. She quickly brushed away that horrible little thought before it took hold. He was probably just Scandinavian. Didn't Scandinavians have really pale eyes?

"Hi, sugar," she purred. "Are you looking for something?"

The man's eyes slid down to her cleavage and back up, his smile fading a bit.

"I am," he said quietly. "Do you have a penis?"

Gloria blinked.

Well, that gets it out of the way. It was slightly off-putting how direct that question sometimes was, but there was something to be said for getting straight to the point.

"I do," she replied, making her grin a little sassier.

"Show it to me."

With a small frown, she straightened.

"That's not the way it works, honey," she said, trying to keep it light. "I'm not putting on a show for free here."

"You'll only do if you have a penis."

Gloria was about to retort, when something occurred to her.

"Oh, honey, did someone pull a fast one on you? Because I am the real deal. Swear to god." She put a hand on her hip and thrust her pelvis forward, using the other hand to smooth the fabric over the small bulge in her crotch. The man's gaze focused on it for a long moment, his strange eyes shrewd.

Truth be told, if he had asked her again, she would have lifted her skirt to show him—she really needed this transaction—but he seemed satisfied enough with her word.

"All right." His words had a clipped quality to them, like he had gone to one of those fancy private schools where they learned archery and had semiformals.

"Your place or mine?" asked Gloria, gesturing to the shitty motel on the corner.

"I have a hotel room," said the man. "Get in."

Normally, Gloria would have one of the other girls take down the license plate of the car before she got in, but there was no one close by. Anyway, she could take care of herself in a fix. The city had set up a rec hall for underprivileged kids, and in her previous life as poor, bullied Gordon, Gloria had taken loads of martial arts classes there; keeping herself safe was not something she worried too much about. Besides, the weird vibes that the john was giving off were almost definitely because he was a rich white guy in a poor neighbourhood, looking to score some action with a black transsexual—Gloria prided herself on being an excellent judge of character, so she shook off her doubts and went around to the passenger side of the big Oldsmobile.

As she slid onto the seat, she let out a happy sigh at how warm it was inside and stretched out her legs to take the pressure off her feet. The car looked like it was from the seventies, at least ten years old, and the legroom was a real treat.

"What's your name?" asked the man after they had pulled away from the curb. His smile had returned, and so had his charm. "I'm Byron."

"Gloria," she replied.

"A beautiful name for a beautiful girl," came the reply.

Yeah, he didn't seem like a bad sort. Gloria grinned at him.

• • •

Byron turned Gloria onto her stomach again and shoved his cock back into her hole to continue fucking her hard. His dick was long, straight, and really stiff, and had an oddly small head. It was like being fucked by the end of a pool cue—all force and no finesse. She winced as he battered her insides and hoped the small groans she wasn't able to stifle would be mistaken for sounds of pleasure. The painful fucking was somehow made worse by the absolute silence on his part.

Gloria closed her eyes for a moment and then let out a cry when his hand worked its way beneath her and grabbed her small, limp cock and *squeezed.*

"Hey, not so hard, sugar!" she gasped, but it was like he hadn't heard her. Gloria's head began to hit the headboard as he pounded into her mercilessly, her dick trapped in his painful viselike hold, and she prayed he would be done soon.

One more minute of this and I'll stop him. Can't treat me so rough. What is taking so long? My poor ass. Lord, I hope the next one is ok with just a blowjob. Fuck, I need the money though—Gloria gritted her teeth at the pain—*Ok... No... I'm so done with this...*

Before she had a chance to try pushing him off her, the man went rigid and let out a quiet little moan.

Finally, thought Gloria and sighed in relief when he pulled his pool-cue cock out of her. She glanced behind her. Byron wiped a hand across his mouth and turned around. His ass was very pale in contrast to the rest of him—everywhere else, he was tanned a golden brown, even though it was mid-January. She watched him walk to the bathroom where he pulled off the condom and took a piss with the door open.

Gloria got to her feet slowly and began fishing around under the bunched coverlet for her purple satin panties. When he spoke directly behind her, she nearly jumped out of her skin.

"I'm sorry. That wasn't very pleasant, was it?" Byron asked. "I took far too long."

"It was fine," Gloria lied, smiling.

"It's because of the breasts, you see."

Gloria frowned.

"The penis is fine… It's the breasts that are wrong," clarified the man with a little shrug. His eyes swept down her body, making her feel strangely self-conscious. "They were distracting. I think I'm a homosexual."

"Oh, honey, it's ok to be gay, you know that right?" said Gloria, feeling a little sympathy for Byron now that he seemed a bit deflated by the confession. He was a weird guy, but even weird guys needed compassion, and she thought of herself as a very compassionate person. She reached out and touched his arm in a friendly way, and he smiled at her.

"Oh, I know. I mean, I think I know," replied Byron. "Thank you for helping me to confirm it, Gloria. Your services are invaluable."

Gloria laughed.

"My pleasure? I guess?" She tried to ignore the pain in her ass as she turned back and leaned over the bed to continue the search for her underwear. "But, I'm going to have to go now, honey. Could you give me a lift back to—"

Gloria was shoved facedown on the bed, and it caught her completely by surprise, so she didn't react right away. The man's knee came down hard on her lower back, and she began to struggle but then felt the sting of a needle in her neck. She let out a yell, trying to force him off of her, but in seconds she could barely move her limbs.

Byron turned Gloria onto her back and peered down at her. She blinked her eyes slowly, trying to make sense of what was happening. He seemed satisfied with her state and leaned out of sight. Gloria managed to turn her head a tiny bit to see what he was doing, and in growing horror, watched him pull a black gym bag out from under the bed. He set it down next to her, and she moaned quietly.

"You're not going anywhere," said Byron, his voice strange and hoarse. "I wasn't finished with you." He rifled through the bag for a moment, pulled out some duct tape, and quickly taped her mouth shut. He crossed the room and turned the TV on—loud music filled the room.

Gloria's heart pounded in her chest, and it was hard to breathe just through her nose. Whatever drug he had injected her with made her feel a bit dopey, but it did nothing to stop the monstrous panic that shrieked inside her.

There was nothing she could do. She couldn't even stop him when he parted her thighs and grabbed her cock brutally hard. Though Gloria was paralyzed, she could feel everything—the pain was excruciating as he crushed her in his fist, his nails digging in. She tried to scream, but between the drugs and the tape, it was just a weak cry.

"You never wanted this, did you?" asked Byron as he frowned at the small, limp dick he held in a tortuous iron grip. He tugged on it hard, as if to rip it off her body, and she let out another little muffled sob. Gloria could feel tears on her face, and her armpits were damp with cold sweat—she panted in pain, and moaned in relief when he let her go. However, when he went back to his black bag and pulled something else out, she began to keen quietly in terror. He held up a scalpel.

"Hush… hush, beautiful," he said gently and reached out to wipe her tears away. "Shhh… It'll be all right." He pushed her legs further apart, and Gloria felt the cold blade touch her right beneath her balls. "I'm just giving you what you've always wanted, that's all. You helped me. I'd like to help you."

Gloria slowly moved her head, trying to shake it, pleading with her eyes. Anything. Anything at all. Anything to stop him.

"I'm going to tell you exactly what I'm going to do to you, my beautiful Gloria. First, I'm going to cut this pathetic, unwanted, sad little penis off your beautiful body. Then, I'm going to make some cuts and open you up"—Byron's breathing became heavier and his face was flushed—"And then I'm going to make *love* to you, Gloria.

I'm going to make you a real woman. I know, I know… You probably didn't imagine your first time as a real woman would be with a gay man. In fact, it might take a really long time for me to achieve orgasm again, but the blood *should* help. Hopefully, you last that long."

Gloria stared at him, terrified.

"You're probably wondering *why* am I going to kill you, aren't you?" said Byron with a smile. The blade nicked her, right near the scar where she'd failed to castrate herself years ago, and she nodded as much as she could.

"Do I really need a reason? I don't really have one other than the thought makes me very happy. *You* should be happy that you're providing yet another invaluable service to me."

Gloria could feel blood running down from the little cut he had made. It would stain the coverlet. She doubted very much that her death would be investigated, and she could just hear her father's voice: "That boy got what was coming to him."

Panic gave way to fury.

I'm a fucking statistic. A stereotype. Another black tranny murdered in cold blood. She wondered if anyone would even claim her body. Then, when the blade cut into her again, she closed her eyes. The music from the TV would cover any sounds she could make. Fury gave way to a deep sadness.

As the scalpel began to slice into her, cutting away her parts, the guttural sounds that came out of Gloria were inhuman.

Byron Anders Danielsen – 1963–2015

Byron stared at Gloria and blinked stupidly in confusion. Was she just some sort of hallucination? It didn't make any sense.

She seemed so *real*.

However, it was truly amazing what a person could make themselves believe—he'd seen it from experience—and without his medication, reality blurred easily.

"I was young and stupid. Rough. She died of her wounds too early," he said of Gloria finally, turning to Michael. The young man sat toying with one of the tracheal dilators on the wheeled metal tray, a pensive expression on his face. "I remember it now. I thought I had lost those memories to the shock therapy…"

"Why do you think you kept her around, so to speak?" asked Michael in a quiet voice.

Byron shrugged. Was it he who had arranged for the bodies to be dragged to the pit beneath the old barn? Was it he who had supervised the hosing down of everything in the bloody sanctuary? Was it he who had been messaging with Michael for the last week? He couldn't remember any of it. But maybe Michael was right— maybe he had only *wished* there were some kind of underground cleaner operation to take care of his messes and a beautiful assistant to arrange everything for him. Maybe pretending to have Gloria around had made things seem more… glamorous. It did make some amount of sense. With each passing moment, he became more convinced—Byron felt clearheaded, like he had on Sepharis before it had interfered with his ability to get an erection and he stopped taking it.

He shifted in his bonds, frowning. But why Gloria in particular? She smiled at him. The gun was lowered at her side.

"I suppose, yes," he answered slowly. "I suppose I keep her 'ghost' here as a reminder of how far I've come. Of my past mistakes. She was my first, you know."

Michael tilted his head.

"That's not what I understand."

"Not my first kill. My first real *sacrifice*," replied Byron. It was the strangest thing to be strapped upright to a table, discussing his murders with a young man who seemed to know incredibly intimate details of his past. The only explanation was that he was having a dream.

"Ah. Right," said Michael with a little nod. "Because there were eight more that you killed before that, I didn't realize you differentiated bet—"

"Seven."

Michael frowned.

"Pardon?"

Byron felt a strange, tight feeling in his guts, and looked over at Gloria again.

"There were seven before Gloria. Not eight."

"Really. Now *that* is interesting."

After placing the dilator carefully back in its place, Michael stood and approached Byron. His dark eyes searched Byron's for a moment, just as they had before.

The tightness inside Byron began to restrict his breathing, and

he panted awkwardly. Michael's face swam in his vision. Familiar…
so familiar.

"Fascinating," murmured Michael, just inches from his face.

Byron flared his nostrils, feeling faint. There were strange light
patterns in Michael's deep brown eyes, his pupils almost overly
large. Byron realized then that he couldn't see himself reflected in
them.

Wake up, Byron. Wake up!

Michael's face split into a wide smile, and he took a step back.
He smoothed his short, dark beard down with a fine-boned hand as
he chuckled to himself.

"You're not asleep, Byron. You're very much awake. I came here
because the powers that be"—he put his hands to either side, palm
up, and looked pointedly skyward—"decided that tonight you must
die. I was just curious to speak with you beforehand. While you
were still in the mortal realm."

"You're insane," said Byron, his eyes wide. He'd thought of
himself as *godlike*, his desires as *sacred*, but a small part of him had
always maintained that those were just words… just silly concepts
that added formality to his play. He didn't *actually* believe them.
Especially now with his head clear. This man standing before him,
however, spoke candidly and with an air of confidence—he *did*
believe what he was saying.

This has to be a dream.

"Really, Byron. When was the last time you had a dream like
this? Hm?" asked Michael, his cheeks dimpling with another coy
smile, obviously enjoying some private joke. "Doesn't this feel just a
little too real to be a dream?"

It was true. When Byron dreamed, his dreams were usually full
of amorphous creatures and indistinct settings. Nothing was ever
clear for more than a moment or two. While everyone else seemed to
dream about flying or winning money or disappointing loved ones,
Byron seemed mostly to dream in the abstract. He had brought it up

with Dr. Abdullah a few times in the twelve years he'd been seeing him, but his therapist had always replied with a noncommittal "that's unusual" and never followed up with any explanation.

Money poorly spent.

"It's not like you're lacking in that department."

Byron lifted his brows.

"If this is not a dream, then how are you doing this? How are you reading my mind? *Who are you?*"

Michael threw back his head and laughed, his teeth white and sharp. Byron felt the tingle of fear again, but more than anything he was getting angry at being toyed with.

"Ok, you little fiend. If you're going to kill me, get on with it. Hm? How are you going to do it? You're going to cut me into pieces? Tear out my guts? Make me *beg*?" growled Byron.

"Oh, nothing like that, *mon cher monstre*," replied the young man with a little headshake. He lifted his hand and placed his warm palm on Byron's chest. "A simple heart attack will do. Imagine what would happen if I tore you apart... What would the cops think of that? This way, there is no doubt that you acted alone when you murdered all those people. Let's give them a little closure, shall we?" He winked.

"How are you going to—" Byron stopped with a strangled gasp. His chest seized with a burning pain, crushing out all breath and squeezing the world down to a point of pure agony.

And then it was over.

CONFUSED, BYRON WATCHED MICHAEL UNSTRAP THE BODY from the table. The middle-aged blond man tumbled to the floor with a cringe-worthy thump and lay there slack-jawed, eyes bugging out. In death, the body was soft and the pose it had landed in was anything but flattering. With a frown, Byron took a step forward. It couldn't be him. He looked small, weak. Pathetic.

Michael looked over his shoulder at Byron as he pulled a

cellphone out of his pocket. With a conspiratorial grin, he held it to his mouth.

"Hello? Hello? Nine-one-one? You gotta help me, man! I don't know how much time I have. This sick fucking dude is trying to kill me! Please… please you gotta—Yeah. Yes! I need help. Listen, this guy is into some really sick shit. Like *sick*, man. Please, he's gonna be back any second. It's like a fucking horror movie in here. So much blood… please…"

Byron stood dumfounded as Michael gave his address to the operator. His gaze kept wandering to the body on the floor…

A slap to his shoulder brought Byron back to his senses, and he looked mutely at Michael. The young man's appearance had changed subtly. His skin was strangely smooth, his eyes more opaque, and when he moved, there seemed to be a reddish haze that followed him… like blood in water.

"That should bring at least one squad car around, I should think," said Michael. He frowned at Byron and then looked over at the dead body. "I admit, that's gotta be weird seeing yourself dead, huh?"

"How… ?" Byron's brain seemed to have abandoned him.

"Loads of time for Q and A later." Michael shrugged, sending a wisp of red curling through the air behind him. "For now, let's just get going, shall we?"

Michael's hand closed over his shoulder.

"Where are we going?" asked Byron softly. The thought that this was *actually* happening to him had started to take root.

"Where do you think?" laughed Michael. "We're going to Hell."

THE DEVIL

If Byron had been expecting a fiery portal to open or some gimmicky whooshing light show, he'd be sorely disappointed —all it took to get back home was a thought. As expected, Byron recoiled when the stark stone walls of Admittance suddenly coalesced around them, and he gaped about in a comical fashion for a moment. Then, as if a steel trap suddenly closed in his mind, Byron's expression went neutral, and he turned to look at him with calm, icy-blue eyes. Why was it always the insane ones who recovered the quickest?

"This is Hell?" asked Byron, lifting one sandy brow. "And who are you… Satan?"

"Satan, the Devil, Beelzebub, Prince of Darkness, Father of Lies, Abaddon, Serpent of Old, Belial, the Morning Star," he rattled off in reply, "and a hundred other names. Personally, I prefer Lucifer. Luce to my friends, but you, my dear, are *not* that. And… don't ever call me 'Lucy.'"

Byron just stared at him for a moment. The man's postdeath shape was a near replica of what he had looked like when alive. He was tall, handsome, well built, and had a subtle haughty tilt to his chin that made Lucifer want to grind him under his heel. Byron's cold eyes appraised his captor as an equal, not as the worm he was, and it sort of pissed him off.

Glancing down at his naked body, Byron frowned.

"Where are my clothes?"

Lucifer laughed and started down the hallway.

"You don't need them here, *carissime monstrum*," called Lucifer over his shoulder. "Come with me."

Byron quickly fell into step as they walked down the long, featureless grey corridor towards the Harrower.

"If you really are who you say you are, isn't continuously calling me 'monster' a case of the pot calling the kettle black?" asked Byron.

Lucifer snorted and nodded once, looking over at his charge. "I suppose so," he admitted.

The serial killer smiled serenely at him and continued on in silence, seeming completely at ease in his nude state as he looked around. Lucifer let his eyes wander down Byron's form. He moved like a dancer—straight-backed with long, measured strides—though Lucifer couldn't recall anything in his profile about lessons. Sometimes it was just a question of innate talent. Byron noticed him looking.

"I feel like I should be flattered by Satan taking me to Hell personally—please forgive me for saying—but this seems a little beneath your station," Byron said pleasantly. "I can't possibly be so evil that the Devil himself has to come calling, can I?"

Lucifer grimaced. "I don't set the rules."

"Who does?"

"You ask a lot of questions."

"I'm just curious. If I'm to be here for eternity, I'd like to know how things work around here."

"You would, would you? Why? Thinking of applying for a job?"

"I always thought that the Devil would be more... intimidating. Frightening. With a keen intellect and a sadistic gleam in his eye. Or at least, I don't know... more *formal?*"

With an exasperated sound, Lucifer stopped in his tracks.

"Listen, Chatty Cathy—no, I don't know why I had to bring you in myself. No, you're not that fucking evil—there are far worse, trust me. No, you're not going to be here for eternity—that's not the point of Hell. And *fuck* you," he growled. "As you so helpfully pointed out: this is *beneath* me. Far, far beneath me. I'm not a fucking tour guide, so *can* it, will you?"

Byron gave a small nod, and the two of them resumed walking. Until Byron passed through the Harrower, Lucifer couldn't lay a hand on him. It was against the rules.

Stupid rules.

When they arrived at the black doors, one of the enforcers stepped up to receive his charge, and Byron's face went white with shock at the sight of the huge, red-eyed demon. With their leathery grey skin, bulging, corded muscle, and massive curling horns, the enforcers made up only about ten percent of Lucifer's workforce, but they were by far the most brutish in appearance.

After giving Byron a cheeky smile as he was dragged through the big doors, Lucifer was finally able to depart. Relieved, he bent reality and *travelled* to his personal office in the lowest level. Sinking down into his comfy desk chair, Lucifer let out a sigh.

He actually didn't blame Byron for all the questions. The whole thing made little sense to Lucifer himself. He was *never* involved personally with the intake process, and he resented being sent like a dog to fetch a new inmate. But what could he do? As he had told Byron, he wasn't the one who made up the rules.

A glass of whiskey appeared in his hand, and he took a sip. At first, he'd thought he'd been assigned to the reaping of Byron's soul because it was too dangerous for any other to handle—a purely evil soul, which was theoretically impossible. But, when 'Michael' had so easily made Byron have doubts about killing him, that idea had flown right out the window.

After a thought, a mirror appeared in his other hand. He looked at himself.

Who are you, Michael? The face and name he'd been given had something to do with Byron's past; that much was obvious.

He remembers seven murders before he started on his psychosexual killing spree, not eight. Were you one of the eight, Michael? The face that stared back at him was of an attractive, almost beautiful man in his midtwenties with black hair and dark eyes. Bearded, he looked like a young Assyrian nobleman—elegant, rather than beastly. He watched himself take another sip of whiskey and then smiled. However, the smile had no humour in it, and all he could think was just how absolutely fucking weary he was. Where once he would have looked forward to the titilating diversion of an intense and perhaps lengthy rehabilitation session with Byron, Lucifer just felt... uninspired.

With that thought, the glass and mirror winked out, replaced by a sheaf of papers. He shuffled through Byron's rap sheet with a frown, each murder and its details laid out in chronological order.

Well, all but one, he thought, looking at the blank sheet that simply said *Michael* at the top. *What* are *you up to, Maker?* When the Almighty remained frustratingly silent on the matter, Lucifer sighed and brought the whiskey back.

It would take the Harrower a while before it was done with Byron, of that he was sure. The job of the ancient machine was to break a new inmate down piece by piece and locate the ungerminated seeds within. Once these were found, the tiny golden molecules of potential Good had to be repaired and readied for growth. Lucifer figured the seeds inside Byron were buried so deep that it would take hours for the Harrower to find them. He had some time on his hands.

Lucifer chose a stapled stack of pages at random—a double murder—and slouched back in his chair to read.

Richard Donovan Kincaid – 1992–2013 / Samuel Jeremy Kincaid – 1994–2013

Sam frowned at the map on his iPhone then looked out the window of the old T-bird at the acres of farmland rolling past. According to Google Maps, the turnoff they were looking for was just up ahead, but it was getting hard to see anything in the falling dusk.

"Are you sure you gave me the right address?" he asked Rick, staring down again at the moving blue arrow on the map. It looked like their destination was sitting in the middle of a field.

His big brother sighed.

"Oh, for fuck's sake, Sammy. Yes. For like the hundredth time. That's the address the dude gave me. He probably lives in an old farmhouse or something. Just keep your eyes peeled, ok, buddy?"

"Yeah, yeah." Sam squinted through the windshield and pointed when a small white sign finally came into sight. "There it is! Fucking hell, why would anyone want to live way the fuck out here?"

Rick just shrugged and turned the wheel. They bumped down

onto the narrow, unpaved road; the T-bird's suspension was a bit stiff, so the ride was a jarring one. Tall trees rose up to either side of the car, making it even darker within.

"This better be worth it," mumbled Sam.

Rick laughed and punched his thigh lightly.

"Will you stop it? I just want to check it out and then we'll hit Tracy's, ok? We'll be fashionably late."

"Seriously, there is *no* way that this guy is for real. A seventy-eight Honda CB750 with less than five thousand miles on it, and he's selling it for *two grand*? He's either insane or fucking stupid."

"Hey, I'll take stupid or insane, as long as it saves me money." said Rick with a grin. "Oh hey… That's gotta be it, right?"

They'd gone up a small hill, and at the end of the road, surrounded by hedges, stood a huge house.

Sam whistled.

"Stupidly *rich*, more like it. Maybe he's got so much money, he doesn't care how much he sells the bike for?"

"Could be."

The midnight-blue T-bird turned onto the circular driveway and stopped in front of the steps. Rick turned the engine off, and the brothers stared up at the colonnaded façade for a few seconds. The car ticked quietly as it cooled.

"But what if he *is*?" said Sam in a small voice. There was something about coming all the way out here that bugged him, and it wasn't just that they'd be late to Tracy's, where he was hoping to sit next to her older brother Greg, thigh pressed to muscled thigh, while they watched the UFC match on Tracy's big-screen TV.

"If he's *what*?" Rick asked, pushing open his door.

"You know… insane," replied Sam. "A psycho?" He got out and stared over the roof of the car at his brother. Rick just rolled his eyes. Though a little shorter, his older brother had the same dirty-blond hair and dark eyes he did. There was no mistaking that they were brothers—in fact, most people assumed they were twins even though they were born over two years apart. However, in contrast to his own tidy appearance, Rick's hair stuck up in its usual shaggy mess, and when he crossed in front of the T-bird to start up the steps, Sam noticed the shirt he had on had a hole near the collar; even worse, his Levis were filthy and ripped above the worn soles of his beat-up Converse sneakers.

Sam shook his head. His brother made no attempt to hide the fact that he was a slob. In contrast, Sam had on what he considered his "date" outfit—skinny jeans with the right amount of fading and a black, collared shirt open over a reproduction vintage Star Wars tee that proclaimed he was both cool and geeky. He brushed his hair out of his eyes and followed Rick up the stairs.

"Think about it, dude. Luring us boys out here to a creepy house so he can do despicable things to us?" Sam realized then that he was only half joking. "Doesn't this feel sort of like a horror movie?"

Rick's hand hovered in front of the knocker for a moment. He looked over at Sam and wrinkled his nose.

"You're such a fucking pussy, you know that?" he said.

"Oh, fuck you." Sam quickly reached past Rick and hammered on the door to show him that he wasn't afraid. His brother smirked and then bumped his shoulder against Sam's. The door opened almost immediately, startling them.

For the size of the house, Sam had been expecting a butler or something, but the middle-aged man who stood in the open door looked nothing like that. He was tall and handsome, with neat blond hair and a welcoming smile on his tanned face. Sam found himself staring like some kind of lovestruck idiot, all thoughts of horror movies punched out of his head by the man's eyes. They were a beautiful, clear, icy-blue—like diamonds…

Do diamonds come in blue? The guy's smile widened the tiniest bit at Sam, and Sam tore his eyes away in shock, cheeks burning. There was absolutely no doubt in his mind about one thing: the guy totally *knew* that Sam was gay, and that both freaked him the fuck out and excited him to no end.

"Can I help you?" said the man in a soft, cultured voice.

"Yeah. We're here about the bike?" replied Rick.

"Of course. You must be Richard. I'm sorry about my surprise. You sounded older on the phone," he explained. "I have to get the keys to the old barn. That's where the motorbike is. Ah… Why don't you come in? We can go through the house."

Sam took another quick look at the guy. He was wearing a loose white shirt, open at the neck, and he seemed like he was in really good shape. When Sam met his eyes again, he was treated to what felt like a private, knowing grin. How did the man know about him? *Nobody* knew. But there was no mistaking the way his eyes slid appreciatively down Sam's body before he turned to lead the boys into the house.

Rick elbowed Sam and leaned closer.

"I think you're giving the old fag a boner, kiddo," he whispered with a smirk.

Sam forced a smile. He hated when Rick acted like a total douche. Rick was actually a nice guy, and really smart too. His best friend. It was just that he *sounded* like a homophobic asshole sometimes. However, he did it often enough that coming out to him was something that Sam wouldn't… couldn't even let himself dream of.

When they stepped over the threshold to follow their host, Sam's heavy heart was left behind as he looked about him in awe. The place was massive with a huge staircase that curled up to a second floor decorated with Greek-looking statues. It was like they were on a movie set.

The man stopped at a small table to one side of the entrance, and he stood rooting through a drawer for a moment.

"I thought I had put the key in here," he said when he came up empty-handed, and his brows pinched together over his nose. "Can I get you boys something to drink while I try to remember where I put the darned thing?" He turned his beautiful blue eyes on Sam, and Sam couldn't stop his brain from pointing out that this guy could be really experienced and would know exactly what he was doing when it came to sex. Being with him would probably be *nothing* like the few awkward, drunken encounters Sam had had so far.

One thing was for certain: the man was making Sam super uncomfortable with his blatant looks. What if Rick noticed... something?

"No tha—" Sam started, but Rick cut him off.

"Yeah sure. Beer?"

What are you doing? He shot Rick a look, but his brother ignored him.

"I only have imported lager, if that's ok?" asked the man pleasantly. When Rick nodded, their host left the room. The air held his cologne for a moment, something subtle and rich smelling.

Rick went in the opposite direction, and Sam reached out to grab his arm.

"Where are you going?"

"I want to look around."

"Don't! He didn't say we could go anywhere."

His brother pulled away.

"What's your problem? I was just going to take a look in the other room," complained Rick. "He offered us beer. It's not like he was going to make us stand here in the hall and drink it, right?" He saw the look on Sam's face and touched his fist to Sam's shoulder. "Oh come on, dude. It's not like I'm going to steal anything. Or... Are you worried about the old pervert touching you? Because I won't let that happen, baby brother. You're safe."

"Safe from what?" asked the man as he walked back into the room carrying two frosted pint glasses of beer.

"Sammy here's a little shy is all," said Rick smoothly, draping his arm over his brother's shoulders.

The older man handed over the beers.

"There's nothing to be shy about... And where are my manners? My name is Byron. I'm really sorry about the keys. I'm sure I'll remember where I put them in a second. Why don't you boys come sit down in the meantime? You can look through the paperwork while you drink your beers."

"Yeah, that's cool," said Rick, and he followed Byron, pulling Sam along.

"I thought we were going to Tracy's," muttered Sam as he sat down next to Rick on the couch. Byron walked to the opposite side of the room and flipped through a folder full of papers.

"We'll be there in plenty of time," replied Rick and took a sip from his glass. He grinned. "Ohhh… This is primo beer. 'Sides… Why are you in such a rush?"

Because this guy is gorgeous and rich, and I'm terrified he's either going to say something incriminating or I'm going to make a fool of myself. Instead, Sam said:

"I was just looking forward to seeing Tracy."

"God, Sammy, why don't you just pull your head out of your ass and actually, you know, *ask her out?*"

"Maybe I will," replied Sam with a scowl and then took a sip of his beer.

Byron found what he was looking for and came back to the couch. He laid out the papers on the big marble coffee table— license information, repair records—and sat down. Rick picked up a creased form and frowned at the writing scrawled across it. Meanwhile, Byron watched Sam curiously. Though the guy had to be in his late forties or early fifties, his face was unlined, and there was a youthful look to him. Sam smiled nervously and glanced down at his beer to watch the bubbles rise to the surface in lines for a moment before taking another tiny swallow. Rick was right; it was really good. However, Sam's bladder had started complaining and neither his nervousness nor the cold beer was helping. He could also use the time to get himself together a bit.

"Can I use your bathroom?" he asked abruptly, interrupting Rick's questions.

"Of course. I'll show you were it is," said Byron, and he rose to his feet.

Oh shit.

Sam's heart thumped hard as he got up off the couch—he hadn't expected Byron to escort him. They were barely around the corner when the older man put his hand softly on Sam's lower back to lead him down the hallway. Unnerved but excited by the contact, Sam closed his eyes and nearly stumbled when his feet hit the edge of the carpet. Byron laughed low, and right then a mental image popped up of him following Sam into the bathroom to kiss him and touch him and *Christ…* Sam was worried he was sweating right through his shirt and Byron could feel it. *Something* was going to happen. Sam could barely breathe.

"It's right through here," said Byron, pointing to a narrow door. Sam rushed past him, terrified but horny as all hell and ridiculously, shamefully confused. He let out a shaky sigh when the door was securely shut.

Sam had just finished washing his hands when the lock turned quietly behind him.

RICK FLIPPED THROUGH THE SHEAF OF PAPERS AGAIN, satisfied that the bike Mr. Money was selling wasn't a piece of shit. He took a gulp of beer, swirled the remaining foam at the bottom, and then finished it. The last bit tasted a little bitter, but that was probably because it was imported beer—they probably didn't have the same standards as America did.

What the fuck is taking so long?

After another few minutes, Rick stood, walked out of the sitting room, and looked down the hallway. Sam and the guy were nowhere to be seen. Rick felt a pang of worry. He'd been joking about the pervert thing, just to tease Sam about what he'd said about the guy being a psycho, but what if he was right?

Don't be stupid.

He frowned and went back to the couch. He would give them five minutes, and if no one came back, he'd go looking for them. After sitting down, he rubbed his face. Rick felt a little weird. He hoped he wasn't coming down with something—he had that shaky sort of feeling he sometimes got at the beginning of a cold. Leaning back against the comfortable cushions, Rick closed his eyes.

HIS EYELIDS WEIGHED A THOUSAND POUNDS, HIS HEAD A hundred times that much. Rick could hear his little brother screaming at him, terrified. He could feel him slapping his face, but it was like a dream, barely there. And there was nothing he could do about it. As darkness swallowed him whole again, he could hear Sam's voice rise in pain then crack as he began to beg.

THERE WAS A HORRIBLE TASTE IN HIS MOUTH AND jackhammers in his head. Rick swallowed hard a few times, then wrenched his eyes open. Thankfully, it was dark, but that meant he had no fucking clue where he was. There was a warm body against him, skin on skin, and when he moved, he heard Sam's voice.

"Oh my god. Oh my god. Thank you god," said his brother. Hands felt his face in the dark, clumsy and grasping.

Rick winced and caught one of Sam's hands.

"What the fuck happened? Where are we?" he asked, groggy and confused.

"I... I don't know. In the house some—somewhere," replied Sam. He was crying.

"Sammy, what's going on?" Rick reached out and put an arm around Sam. He realized that they were both naked. A breathless sob shook his brother's skinny frame.

That sick fuck.

"Oh, Rick. It's bad. Ssso"—it was a few seconds before Sam's crying stopped long enough for him to speak—"so *fucking* bad."

Anger boiled up in Rick, and he squeezed Sam's shoulder hard.

"Did he touch you? What did he do to you?" When Sam wouldn't answer, he shook his little brother. "Did that fucker *touch* you?"

The lights turned on right then, and the pain in Rick's head screamed in protest.

"I didn't do anything to him, Richard. Well… not much." Their host walked up to a big old-fashioned chair and sat down, smiling peacefully and wearing nothing but a red robe. They were in a round room with wooden walls, and Rick and Sam were on a platform of some sort.

Rick struggled to his feet.

"I'm going to fucking *kill* you." However, he had only taken one step before he was stopped by his brother's strangled cry: "Don't!"

Byron picked up something from his lap and smirked.

"Listen to your brother, Richard, if you don't want to accidently kill him."

Rick looked behind him but didn't understand what he was seeing at first. Sam was on his knees with some sort of metal contraption around his neck, tears running down his face. There was a new bruise blossoming on one of his cheeks. Confused, Rick turned to Byron and saw that the thing in his hand was a remote.

"What the fuck is going on?" he asked, his heart racing.

"Simply put: If you don't do what I say, your brother dies," replied Byron. "If you try to come any closer, your brother dies. If you try to escape, your brother dies. If you even touch the collar around his neck… dear, sweet Samuel dies."

"How?" Rick's voice was quiet and calm though his mind was tripping over itself in a panic.

"I push this button, and a lethal dose of potassium chloride gets delivered directly into his bloodstream, stopping his heart. I hear it's very, very painful."

Rick glanced back at Sam and saw that his little brother's eyes were wide with terror. The pain in his head receded into the distance. His breathing slowed. His mind settled on one thing: protect Sam at all cost.

"What do I do?" he asked, meeting the eyes of their tormentor.

Byron chuckled softly and crossed one leg over the other. The robe slipped open, and Rick could see the guy's dick—he was sporting a semi.

Fucking pervert.

"You're going to put on a little show for me," said the older man with a tiny head tilt. His eyes were flat and cold like a corpse's. "You simply have to do one thing for me, and if you do it well and impress me, I'll let you go."

"What?" growled Rick, getting impatient with the way the fucker was drawing it out.

"Easy. I want to watch you have sex with your brother."

No. No, no, no, no. Behind him, Sam choked and began to sob again.

"That is *sick* dude. That isn't—" Rick stopped when Byron held up the remote, his thumb hovering over one of the buttons; he put up his hands in supplication. "Ok, ok… *easy* now. No need for that. I just—" He looked at Sam. The younger boy was trembling with his head down. "Shit… I just don't know if it's *possible*. I don't think I'm physically capable of—"

"I have Cialis… Viagra… Levitra. There are ways of making it happen, believe me."

Rick's nostrils flared. He was pissed, but mostly he was terrified. The guy was absolutely serious, of that he was sure.

"So, if I fuck him, you're going to let us go? That's the deal? What guarantee do I have?"

"I can give you my word, but I know that's not enough, is it? Well… The only thing I can think of is this: *what choice do you have*? I'm not asking you to kill him. I'm asking you to show him a few tender moments of brotherly love. You can do that, can't you?"

Sickened by his fear to the point of nausea, Rick sank down to his knees on the platform and held his head between his hands, breathing deep. Sam's arm came around his waist, and he felt his brother's wet face against his side.

Could he do this thing? This horrible, twisted thing? This… perversion that he'd dreamt of once, a long time ago. A dream that was burned into his brain: Sam beneath him, panting, moaning, body between his hands slick with sweat. He'd never told anyone about it. Couldn't.

"Can you give my brother and me a few minutes in private?" He met the cold, dead eyes with desperation. "Please?"

Byron's brows furrowed for a moment, but then he nodded. He rose to his feet.

"I will give you a moment since you asked so nicely. Don't do anything stupid." The man left the room with a whisper of silk. "I have something to take care of anyway."

Quickly, Rick reached for the collar Sam wore, but his little brother recoiled.

"Don't!"

"It's ok. I'm not trying to take it off. I just want to see—" Rick fiddled with the device but couldn't tell what was keeping it closed. He couldn't chance messing with it too much. What if there was a fail-safe?

"Ricky, I am so fucking scared," said Sam in a weak voice.

"It's going to be *fine*. It'll be ok. This sick pervert's just watched *Saw* too many times. I'll get us out of here."

Sam nodded, wiping his nose on his wrist. His eyes were bright red from crying, and his normally smooth wing of dirty-blond hair was a limp, tangled mess that hung over his face.

"You can do it," whispered Sam. "To… to me."

"Shut up. No one's gonna do *that* to you," replied Rick, looking around the room searching for a weapon. Anything.

"No. It's ok. He'll let us go, right? Just... just... pretend I'm a... a beautiful blond with big tits and an ass that tastes like French vanilla ice cream." Sam swiped at his nose again, a scared smile on his face.

The suggestion was so ludicrous that Rick choked out a laugh despite himself. It was a fucked-up, bullshit, horrible situation, and Sam was quoting *True Romance*.

"I think he's bluffing about the, uh... chlorium... pots... shit," said Rick. "And if he's not, what makes you think he'll let us go? I... I just"—Rick had to take a few breaths or else he would start bawling his eyes out too—"don't want to hurt you."

"You're not," said Sam, averting his gaze. "It doesn't hurt like that. Not if you go slow. I've... I've done it before."

"Why? Did Tracy let you..." Rick trailed off when Sam's wide brown eyes met his. "Oh."

Thing was... He'd known about Sam for a long time. Since they were little kids, really. He'd just hoped that...

What? That you could un-gay him?

He stared at Sam for a moment, his jaw clenched tight.

"So, you're a homo," he said finally. "Who cares? Right?" He grabbed Sam by the shoulders and pulled him into a tight hug. "I still love you, buddy. 'Kay? No matter what happens."

"How lovely."

Rick turned and scowled at Byron. His robe hung open, and his dick swayed as he walked back to his seat. Rick would make him *pay*. He'd rip that fucking psycho pervert a new one...

"Are we ready then, boys?" said the man as he sat down. He held up the remote, a smile on his face. "Or are we going to have a tragic demise?"

Rick quickly murmured to Sam as he gave him another tight hug.

"Ok, we'll put on a little show, and he's going to get distracted, and that's when I'm going to get him. Just... these things I'm going to do to you. I'm going to say things… but, just remember: it's not me and it's not you, right? *Right?*"

Sam nodded, his face bleak.

"I'll be ok."

After a deep breath, Rick pushed Sam away at arm's length. He looked over at Byron with a scowl.

"You don't expect me to fuck him without lube, do you?" he growled.

Their host chuckled.

"No, of course not. On the table next to you."

Rick looked up and saw the clear bottle on the kind of metal table that normally featured in operating rooms—it was even covered in a square of green, absorbent-looking paper, just like in the movies. He picked up the bottle and pumped a few squirts into his hand.

"Sammy, go down on your hands and knees." Rick couldn't believe this was happening. It was monstrous… Yet the sight of his brother naked, on all fours, was doing something to him. Sam's ass was narrow and bony, and there was a tiny pimple on the left cheek, but the way his asshole was right there, presented to him. Rick dropped to his knees behind Sam and put the bottle down next to him. He lubed up his cock quickly, trying to hide his growing erection, not wanting to let the psycho fucker have the satisfaction of seeing that he was getting hard so easily.

I'm a goddamn sicko, he thought, squeezing himself. He glared at Byron. *But he's worse.* "Enjoying yourself?" Rick said with a sneer.

Byron's dick was still only at half-mast in his lap; the older man shrugged and motioned for Rick to continue.

Rick pumped another few squirts onto his fingers and reached for Sam. He stalled just before touching his ass, but then he clenched his teeth and forced himself to smear the lube onto himself and then into his brother. Sam's breath hitched.

"Sorry. A little cold," he muttered quietly. The sight of his finger breaching Sam's hole made his dick throb in his fist.

Sick sick sick sick.

He stroked himself a few more times.

"Remember what I said, Richard. You have to impress me… So take your time."

Fuck you, you fucking fucker.

Rick shuffled forward on his knees and pointed his dick at Sam's shiny, wet asshole. Then, with one hand on Sam's hip, he pulled his brother slowly back towards him until he made contact. A strangled, involuntary groan came from him as he watched his cockhead push against his brother's pucker. He wanted to close his eyes. Wanted to imagine he was fucking Lisa or Karine or any one of the girls who he sometimes flirted or hooked up with. Anything but watch himself slowly slide his cock into his little brother's tight asshole. But he couldn't look away. Beneath him, Sam tensed and let out a quiet, pained noise. Instead of making him stop, the sound *pulled* at the sickness inside him and he pushed harder.

"Uhhhfffuck," whimpered Sam as his ass took more of Rick's rock-hard dick. "Ow."

Rick let go of his cock to hold Sam's narrow waist with both hands, and he thrust himself in the rest of the way. Sam tried to move forward on his knees to get away from the sudden, deep penetration, but Rick held him in place.

Then he started to fuck Sam with quick strokes.

Forgive me.

"You like that? Hm, Sammy boy? Lookit how easy you take my big cock, you little slut. You were craving a good deep-dicking from your big brother all these years, weren't you? I should have fucking known." Sam's ass squeezed hard at his dick, hot and slick. Rick panted a few breaths and looked at Byron. The man was stroking himself, his eyes glittering with sick lust at the spectacle. "Is this what you wanted? You wanted to watch me plug my kid brother's ass with my big, thick cock? You sick fuck. You probably want to hear him cry some more, don't you?"

Byron's lips stretched into a wide smile.

Rick pounded into Sam, hating himself for needing so little encouragement. He reached forward and grabbed the back of Sam's hair in his fist and slammed his cock home a few more times. He was getting close fast. Just the thought of filling Sam's ass with his cum…

Sam cried out, his body shaking and twitching to get away from Rick's brutal fucking. Rick knew he was hurting.

You wanted a show, you sick fuck? Well, I'll give you a fucking show. He curled his lip and grunted in time with his thrusts. *Distract him. He'll put down the remote and then I'll get him.*

When they got out of this, and they *would* get out of this, Rick would give Sammy his car. Shit, he would let him punch him in the face as hard and as many times as he wanted. He would be his slave for the rest of his life.

Rick watched his shaft sliding in and out of Sam's ass, his cock veiny and shiny with lube, and knew he would only last a few more thrusts. His sack was tight over his balls… the sweet, sweet promise of release like a warm honey glow in his groin.

"Fuck," he huffed out between breaths, his cock going like a piston, ignoring the way that Sam cried out with every thrust.

Rick was so distracted that he didn't feel the knife at his throat until it was too late. The blade didn't even hurt… He was too caught up in the throes of climax, pumping his cum deep into his brother's body with every plunge. Sam's terrified scream did nothing to help, his ass squeezed Rick's dick even harder as he was covered with hot splashes of blood. It all happened so fast.

As he slumped down onto Sam, dick slipping wetly out of him, all he could think about was how he had failed him. Then there was nothing at all.

Sam struggled to get out from under Rick, screaming then gagging as hot gouts of blood poured into his mouth when he turned his head. Hands grabbed him roughly by the shoulder, and he felt Rick's body pushed off of him. Then Sam howled in pain as his ass was speared brutally by something long and hard. It took him a second to realize that it was a cock and that he was being raped. The pain was intense. It felt like his insides were being ripped open as the man above ploughed into him again and again.

Rick! Where's Rick?

Blood. Pain. It went on for a long time. Sam retreated into his mind, flopping forward numbly in the cooling puddle of gore with every thrust. Finally, the man let out a grunt and pushed inside him hard and stayed still for a moment. Then it was over.

Sam weakly turned onto his side and curled into the foetal position. Rick lay within arm's reach, his eyes wide and sightless—the cut on his neck was like a second bloody, grinning mouth. He wanted to cry. He wanted to scream. But Sam did nothing but lie there motionless, reeling from the shock of what had just happened. He heard the sound of someone walking around, humming along to the soft classical music that played. Then there were gentle hands on him, turning him over. Crystalline blue eyes looked into his. There was a kind smile on the man's face... as if nothing had happened. As if it were all a dream.

"You can go now," said the man in a friendly voice.

Sam blinked a few times. The man helped him up, and he sat there in a stupor, oblivious to the pains, both inside and out.

"Samuel," said Byron with another smile. He brushed Sam's hair out of his eyes. "You can go. It's over."

As if in a trance, Sam climbed to his feet, holding the man's arm. His fingers crept up to his throat hesitantly.

"C-collar?" Sam's voice was hoarse, and it came out as a croak.

"You can take it off now. The clasp is under your left ear."

"But"—he didn't dare touch it—"the potassium chloride..."

Byron laughed low, just as he had in the darkened hallway and again when he had surprised Sam in the bathroom. The man reached out, touched the collar, and with a *click*, it fell to the floor.

"You were never in any real danger, my dear boy. It's nothing but a stage prop."

"But… but…" Tears started streaming down Sam's cheeks. His whole body ached.

"Go on now, Samuel. You're free. Go on home."

The spell was broken, and Sam shot forward, running past the madman. He slipped in blood, landed on one knee with a pained grunt, but recovered in an instant. Naked, covered in gore, and with something slimy and wet he couldn't think about leaking down between his thighs, Sam ran through the house and burst out the front door. There he stopped in confusion. Where was the car?

Panting in terror, Sam glanced back at the house and saw that Byron stood in the doorway, a sly smile on his face.

"Oh. I'm afraid your car may have driven itself into the swamp out back," said the older man. How could Sam have ever thought his eyes were beautiful? The cold, dead eyes stared at him, mocking his fright.

With a sob, Sam took off at a sprint down the narrow, tree-lined road. Gravel tore into his feet as he ran, but he didn't care. He just had to get to the highway. Maybe from there he could wave someone down. He'd get the police. He'd been raped… There was *proof*… and…

Oh my god, Rick.

A horrible stuttering, wailing sound poured out of him as he ran. His brother. His hero. The grunting at the end, hands digging into his sides, cock deep inside him… For a shameful second it had felt almost good. Then the blood… The way Rick's body had jerked about on top of him.

Oh god. Oh god.

His lungs were on fire, his feet torn to ribbons, but he was going to make it. The road wasn't that long. He would make it—

Sam pitched forward and skidded to a painful, bloody halt on the dirt road, his limbs twisted beneath him. Something had hit him hard in the ass and knocked him to the ground. There was a metallic taste in his mouth. Weirdly groggy, he craned his neck and saw what looked like a dart sticking out of his left butt cheek. He tried to reach for it, but his arm wouldn't obey.

By the time Byron walked up, holding the tranquilizer gun against his shoulder and looking terribly amused, Sam could barely keep his eyes open.

Oh god.

"That *was* rather mean of me, wasn't it?" laughed Byron, squatting down next to Sam's head. He turned to speak to someone else just out of sight. "No, Gloria. That's the point... I had no intention of actually letting him loose. You really have no sense of humour, do you?"

Sam blinked slowly, his panic trapped inside a body that wouldn't move. Though he couldn't hear the woman's reply, he could hear Byron just fine.

"Let's get him back to the sanctuary... I was nowhere near done."

It was days until Sam finally gasped his last pain-filled breath.

LUCIFER LET OUT A LOW WHISTLE WHEN HE'D FINISHED THE detailed account of the boys' deaths and put the pages facedown on his desk. Byron was a real, twisted piece of shit. With a deep frown, Lucifer pondered for a moment—he thought of a pair of reapers that would probably work well to play the part of Rick and Sam. He wondered suddenly if the demons were brothers.

Brothers... How fitting would that be? Lucifer smiled. Brothers or not, the important thing was that reaper demons were vicious in their sadism, and the fact that the breed had sharp barbs on their cocks was just bloody icing on the torture cake. Lucifer mentally checked that the demons were available for when the Harrower would be done with Byron, and when the confirmation came, he settled more comfortably into his seat.

He took another sip of whiskey and side-eyed the pages on his desk. Then he closed his eyes, rested his head back against the chair, and shook his head slowly, his lips pressed tight.

Don't.

Lucifer turned his chair away from the pages to face the big window where he could watch the various goings-on below. After a minute or so, he swivelled back around and tried to busy himself with some mundane paperwork over a gang rape in rural India. However, he kept catching himself glancing at the pages containing Rick and Sam's story.

You can't.

Lucifer gritted his teeth and tried to focus, but it was impossible. He leaned over his desk and drummed his fingers on the boys' account, with eyes narrowed and forehead wrinkled.

You're the sick piece of shit.

Chastising himself didn't help, of course. Hell did strange things to him... everything he had seen and done—it was impossible to get away from it. Truth was that he belonged here every bit as much as Byron did.

With a sigh, Lucifer finally turned the stack of papers over. He quickly undid his button and zipper and slid his hand into the opening. Lucifer shifted in place to get better access to himself, and with a guilty, shameful feeling in the pit of his stomach as he squeezed his cock, he flipped back a few pages, found the spot he was looking for, and began to read it over from there:

"It was monstrous... Yet the sight of his brother naked, on all fours, was doing something to him. Sam's ass was narrow and bony, and there was a tiny pimple on the left cheek, but the way his asshole was right there, presented to him..."

A LIVING HELL

Byron woke up sprawled out on his stomach on a hard surface. Confused, he lifted his head and saw that he was on the floor of a small room with smooth, curved walls. Light bathed him in a warm glow, but there was no source in sight.

Slowly, he pushed himself up to a sitting position, trying to make sense of where he was. The realization that he was naked triggered a rush of memories: being drugged and restrained by Michael, the heart attack, walking down a strange hallway… the demon… the monstrous *thing*—

"Oh god," he whispered and pressed the back of his hand to his lips as he recalled the horror. The way it had pulsed and whined like a great, living machine made of hot, slimy skin and sharp metal blades. His demon escort—the impossible, bestial creature with corpse-grey skin and eyes like bleeding ulcers—had pushed him into the *thing's* stinking embrace. The machine had clung to him, as possessive as a lover, while its razors peeled away layer after layer of his viscera. Digging, searching inside him for something—the unending, terrible *pain*. He closed his eyes and breathed deep. How was he still alive?

That's right… I'm not *alive, am I?*

If he was to believe Michael, he was literally in Hell, and Michael was not a handsome young man in his midtwenties with a taste for fine wine and backseat fellatio, but the Lord of Flies himself. Byron rubbed his face and chuckled to himself. He'd gone insane—finally and completely insane.

Byron got to his feet and looked around. The walls were blank, totally unrelieved by door or window, and they were slightly warm to the touch—almost as if they were alive. Unnerved by that thought, he wiped his hand on his naked hip and took a step back.

If he was insane and this was all just a construct of his fractured mind, then shouldn't he have *some* control over his surroundings? Byron closed his eyes and pictured his sanctuary, but when he looked again, he was still in the strange, featureless room. As a construct, it was pretty solid.

He was just wondering what he was expected to do if he needed to use the facilities, when someone else was suddenly in the room with him. Despite the fact that Michael's appearance was disturbingly abrupt, Byron felt only mildly put out rather than shocked. There was something irritating about the fact that the younger man was tastefully dressed in a pair of well-tailored black dress pants with a subtle white-on-white damask dress shirt open at the neck while he stood there in nothing but his skin. Curling his lip, he met Michael's dark, long-lashed eyes with an icy stare and crossed his arms.

"So good of you to join me," he said.

His captor smiled and sat down on the chair that had apparently materialized alongside him. He gestured for Byron to do the same, and after making sure a chair was actually behind him, Byron sat down. The contoured wood seat was uncomfortably cold on his bare posterior.

Michael lounged back and appraised him.

"You know, I have to admit I'm amazed you're awake already. The Harrower really had to dig for—"

"Why am I here?" asked Byron, cutting him off.

Michael leaned forward in his chair. The movement was echoed by the reddish streaks that flowed in the air around him, and he fixed Byron with a look of barely contained amusement.

"You're shitting me, right?"

Byron frowned.

A wrinkle appeared on Michael's smooth brow, and he stroked his glossy, short black beard down.

"You didn't honestly think you were going to get off scot-free after killing nearly fifty people, did you?" he said, sounding incredulous. "You're in Hell, buddy. Right where you belong."

"And you're the Devil."

"And I'm the Devil. The sooner you get that through your head, the sooner we can get started."

"Started… what, exactly?" Byron didn't like the way Michael—or Lucifer—rolled his eyes. It was disrespectful. Everything about him was *disrespectful*. Then, his mind played back the memory of the meal they'd shared at *Le Clin d'Oeil*; the gorgeous view afforded by the well-placed table completely wasted on them as the lively and intelligent conversation claimed their full attentions. That young man, clever and eloquent, was nothing like this egoistic, rude—

Byron tilted his head when his thoughts didn't elicit a reaction from the Devil.

"You can't read my mind anymore," he guessed.

Lucifer's lips pressed together for a moment, and something dark passed over his expression.

"I can't," he agreed in a quiet voice.

"Because you don't make the rules. Isn't that what you said earlier before you handed me off to that creature?"

"Correct."

"And who does? *God?*" Byron couldn't hold back his mocking smile.

With nostrils flared slightly, Lucifer let out a frustrated breath.

"*Enough.* I was going to let you have more time to recover

before we started your rehabilitation, but since you seem to be in *such* fine spirits, I think we can jump right into it." He stood and the chairs disappeared, dumping Byron unceremoniously to the ground.

However, before Byron had a chance to get back on his feet, two young men appeared out of thin air and fell upon him. In seconds they had Byron immobilised in a metal apparatus that had him on elbows and knees with legs spread, unable to move even his head for the tight collar around his neck. Byron knew it well—after all, he was the one who had designed the rape stand.

The young men stood looking down at him; one in a worn T-shirt and dirty jeans, the other considerably better dressed. They looked enough alike that strangers mistook them for twins, but Byron knew that they weren't. He took a few short breaths as his heart seemed to flutter in his chest.

The older one is Richard, or Rick *to his younger brother Sam.*

"See, in Hell there is punishment, yes—but the name of the game is *rehabilitation*." Lucifer was somewhere off to his right. No matter how hard Byron tried, he couldn't see the man. "The Harrower found seeds of remorse, compassion, sympathy, etcetera inside you, but they were buried really fucking deep—deeper than I've seen in some time. Right now, what we need to do is stimulate growth in those seeds, Byron. Do you understand? We need to make you *whole* so you can move on into the Light." The Devil's hand slid down Byron's back softly, his fingers hot against his skin. "But… Those seeds were in the dark for *such* a long time that they hadn't even started to germinate yet. Because of that, we have to begin with the very basics. And do you know what those are?"

Byron stared at the two boys. Were they actually Richard and Samuel Kincaid? Were they demons? Lucifer's hand stroked his head, gentle for a moment, and then he grabbed a handful of hair and twisted until Byron gasped in pain—his hair follicles screamed in agony as some were ripped from his scalp.

"Pain!" he finally blurted out, and the hand loosened its grip.

"Good," purred the Devil. "Pain and… ?"

Heart racing, Byron thought quickly—what did Lucifer want to hear? The brothers smiled at each other fiendishly as they reached for their zippers. The huge, half-erect members they pulled out had wide, dark heads and strangely ridged shafts. Byron tried to breathe normally as the boys, with smug looks on their handsome faces, began to stroke themselves ramrod stiff in front of him. Then the younger one threw back his head and clutched himself hard at the base. In horrified fascination, Byron watched the backwards-facing barbs lift from the taut, swollen skin. The older brother's shaft bristled with its own curved spikes a moment later, and when a pearly bead emerged from the slit in his glans and stretched out in a long drip that broke off, it hit the floor with a curl of pale smoke; Byron thought he heard a soft hiss when a second drop fell.

He had to lick his lips and swallow the dryness away before he could answer. Byron knew *exactly* what Lucifer wanted him to say.

"Fear," he said in a hoarse voice. Those barbs would shred his insides, and there was no telling what their semen would do to him. The younger brother grinned at him. "Pain and fear."

"That's right," said Lucifer with a chuckle. "Pain and fear. Those will be your first lessons, and you will learn them well. Boys?"

Gasping for breath, Byron tensed in his restraints. He lost sight of the brothers as they circled behind him.

"You can't be serious…" Byron's voice was almost shrill. "This can't… I don't understand how this is *rehabilitation*? You *have* my fear. You win! I'm afraid. But… You… You can't *do* this!" Byron's panic was a wild creature caught in a snare, chewing its own leg off. "No—" He felt something stroke the back of his thigh, and the skin there twitched involuntarily, as if his very flesh was trying to flee.

"I *am* serious. I know I have your fear—and I thank you for that—but you're only just tasting the beginning of what fear can do to you. I find that a good, firm grasp on fear and pain helps to create fertile ground for proper rehabilitation and personal growth… But don't take my word for it. I just work here."

"But th-this isn't how it happened with those boys!" Byron couldn't keep the pain out of his voice as a rough, dry finger probed his anus.

At least I gave Richard lubricant… He didn't dare say it. Lucifer appeared in his field of vision and crouched in front of him so he could look him in the eye.

"You brought this upon yourself, Byron," said the Devil, his tone almost intimate. Then there was a brief second of respite from the demon brothers' rough fondling, enough that Byron could focus on the man in front of him. For a moment, he thought he saw something like sorrow soften Lucifer's eyes, but when the younger man's insolent smile returned in the next instant, Byron thought he had probably imagined it. With a tiny bow of his head, the Devil winked out of sight, the red-streaked mist that shadowed his every movement lingering in the air for a breath longer.

"Wait!" Byron called in a strangled voice.

Struggling in vain against the metal restraints that bound him, Byron groaned as one the demon brothers finally positioned himself between his parted knees. His fear was worse for having been abandoned by Lucifer—it had become abject terror at his departure.

And who is he? Your ally? Your friend? The thought sent a bubble of hysterical laughter to his lips, but it erupted as a full-throated cry instead as the demon penetrated him to the hilt in one vicious thrust. As bad as the pain was with the first plunge, it paled in comparison to the all-consuming agony that tore through Byron as the demon pulled back, the spines on his cock ripping deep furrows inside him.

Eventually, the lining of Byron's oesophagus tore from sustaining the unending scream that poured from his throat, and he died with the taste of blood in his mouth.

Lucifer stood over Byron's body. He lay crumpled in a gigantic puddle of blood, and all that was left of his ass was a huge, gaping wound; Lucifer thought he could see the white curve of his pelvic bone in the wreckage. Squatting down on his haunches, Lucifer peered into Byron's lipless face, the skin melted off entirely in places. With his eyes narrowed at the remains of Byron, Lucifer remained there a little while, trying to figure out what it was that felt *wrong*.

RINSE, REPEAT

Byron woke up sprawled out on his stomach on a hard surface. Again.

With a frown, he lifted his head and saw that he was still in a featureless room—thankfully alone. He rubbed his face and sat up. As far as he could tell, he was completely intact. The only thing that remained of the terrible, endless pain was the memory of it. He clenched his jaw and leaned forward for a few seconds, nauseous and a bit faint.

He didn't know how many times the demon brothers had raped him, but his calves and forearms had become covered with his blood as it ran across the floor in sluggish rivulets. Byron remembered a little part of him, locked away from the gibbering, inhuman thing that pain had turned his mind to, had been aware enough to be thankful that the apparatus he was locked into didn't allow for the two of them to penetrate him at once.

Wiping his mouth, Byron shakily got to his feet. The floor was the same noncolour as before, somewhere between grey and beige, and there was no trace of what had happened. With nowhere to sit, and nothing to distract him from his memories, Byron began to pace.

If this is Hell, I cannot die, he reasoned. *I have already died, and my body is probably sitting in a morgue somewhere as law enforcement picks through my home.* He clenched his jaw at the thought of all those hands touching his belongings but after another circuit of the room, felt his anger begin to fall away, replaced by curiosity about his situation. *If I have already died, then I cannot experience mortal pain, can I? The fear of death is what drives man to succumb to his pain—fear weakens the resolve. Without the fear of death, what is left?*

Byron stopped pacing and stood staring into space, his mind sorting through the possibilities. It was something he'd already pondered at length: how many painful, humiliating, horrifying things could you make a person do if they thought they would survive it? In Hell, there was no surviving, because there was no death. The only fear, really, was the fear of pain itself. How long could you keep your hand in boiling water if, somehow, you were made to believe that there would be no injury?

Before he'd lost his license due to malpractice, it was something he had been testing… to varying results. Byron resumed walking, measuring his steps so they echoed in the room like a clock ticking. It was an interesting predicament indeed.

Fear is all in the mind. Yet, I am all *mind here, am I not? That little fiend means to see me succumb to my fear so that I may become, what? A better person?* Byron smiled. Since it was simply a question of mind over matter, something that should be easily achieved considering the lack of *actual* matter, he pushed the subject of his own fear and pain aside for the moment and turned his thoughts to his jailer.

Tired of going in circles, Byron stopped and looked around in frustration—the lack of furniture was irritating and was surely a tactic to wear him down. With a sigh, he sat down on the smooth, hard ground. Then Byron closed his eyes and pictured Lucifer as he had looked moments before he had left him to be tortured: soft brown eyes, dark brows low… a tiny twitch of his lips. Sympathy? Sadness? Byron frowned. Not quite right. *Weary.* Was that why he had left? Tilting his head, Byron let his mind wander down that path. Could the Devil get weary of his work? Was it a chore to supervise his so-called rehabilitation? Did participating *bore* him? Again, it didn't feel right. Byron had spent his entire life studying the tiny changes in human expression, and though Lucifer was not in fact human, his face was just as expressive—something seemed *off* about the flippant remarks and cheerful indolence... Byron opened his eyes. Was it that the Devil no longer had the heart to do what he did?

"That's an interesting thought," he said.

"What is?" Lucifer's voice startled him, but Byron turned with a smile as if he'd known he was there.

Lucifer was dressed in dark blue jeans, a white T-shirt, and a slate-grey blazer. He was perfectly handsome, and his smile had none of its usual mocking quality—for a moment Byron saw only the young man who had kissed him almost shyly in front of the French bistro while they waited for Byron's driver to bring the car around. His beard had been soft on Byron's palm, his mouth sweet from the port they had drunk. Byron remembered the graceful curve of his back that led to the taut roundness of his ass. The little sound of pleasure when Byron had pulled Michael firmly against him...

Not *Michael.*

Byron realized his smile had slipped a tiny bit.

"I was just contemplating the nature of my incarceration," he said in reply to Lucifer's question.

"Oh? And did you come to any conclusions?" As he had the day before, the Devil brought a couple of chairs into existence. They sat facing each other, and Byron made a show of being unselfconscious of his nakedness, but it chafed him to be kept at a disadvantage. Not that he was uncomfortable with everything being on display. Byron had a great body for a man his age, and he knew it. It was just that, like the lack of furniture, the forced nudity was another means of subjugating him. He crossed one leg over the other, ankle resting on the knee opposite, and put his hands on the armrests. The leather chair was a graceful art deco piece, and Byron wondered whether the choice of it reflected Lucifer's taste or if he was simply trying to impress him.

"No conclusions," said Byron with a tiny shrug, "just more questions."

"Ah."

"Like: Why are we talking right now? Is this part of the process? Are you trying to gauge my response to your so-called rehabilitation techniques?"

Lucifer stared off to the side, his expression unreadable. Byron leaned forward a touch.

"I don't get why you didn't just give me a heart attack at the restaurant instead of sitting there with me for over two hours. For that matter… Why come out with me at all? Did your god make you do it?"

The Devil turned his dark eyes to him and frowned. "Xe's your god too."

"Zee?"

"Xe. With an *X*. It's a gender-neutral pronoun. Where have you been living? Under a rock?"

Byron ignored the remark.

"So, is that a yes, then? You slavishly do everything you're told? I always thought the Devil ran Hell, but you're really just middle management, aren't you?" Provoking Lucifer probably wasn't the smartest thing to do, but as he spoke, he realized something surprising. He was angry not just at being forced to submit to some god he didn't believe in… But something about having been betrayed by Michael struck a chord inside him.

Not Michael. Never Michael. Michael would never—

Byron blinked rapidly a few times, trying to hold onto the tiniest sliver of a memory, but then it was gone. He shook his head and focused on Lucifer. The Devil was smoothing his beard slowly with one hand while he stared at him.

"You said you cannot read my mind because it's against the 'rules,' but could you do it if you *broke* the rules? Or are you too afraid?" asked Byron.

"Are you done?" replied Lucifer, his face impassive.

"Answer one question," Byron said with a smile, "and I will be done, yes."

"Which one? You're just full of questions." The Devil's tone was light, but it seemed forced.

"Just this: was it all an act?" Byron asked, watching him carefully. "At the restaurant?"

"Of course it was," replied the Devil, scowling. "I was just testing a hypothesis. And no, the date was not the Almighty's idea; it was mine."

"What hypothesis? That I would kill you? That's not much of a hypothesis given my history. But… You *knew* my thoughts. You had to have seen that I was planning on letting you go, yet you pressed on, knowing that if you stepped inside my home, I would end your life… Why?"

"It was the inevitable conclusion."

"Not so. I really would have let you live."

Lucifer's expression took on a slightly guarded cast. He drummed his fingers on the curved arm of the chair.

"You want to know why," said Byron.

"Yes," admitted the Devil after a slight pause.

"Interesting. You could read my thoughts but not my intentions." Byron sat back in his chair, feeling like he had a tiny advantage—for the moment at least. "And I could keep that information from you now, if I so wished, because of what seems like a rather asinine rule to have here in Hell. Wouldn't it benefit you to know whether your charges were lying to you or not? In fact," Byron said, shaking his head, "that rule makes absolutely no sense. Unless"—he searched Lucifer's eyes—"it's only *me* that you cannot read." He got confirmation when a small wrinkle appeared between the Devil's black eyebrows.

"Are you going to make me torture it out of you?" asked Lucifer, ignoring his questions.

"Do you *want* to torture it out of me?" Byron replied, but he continued after a beat, not giving Lucifer a chance *not* to answer. "But no, you don't have to… I'll tell you right now. Simply put, I was charmed by what I perceived as a gentleness of character. Something truly *good*. Even I falter in the face of such a rarity."

"If you're trying to butter me up, you're wasting your time," said Lucifer, rising out of his chair. He took a step back, and two figures coalesced in the air in front of him. Byron was confused for a moment. There was one of the boys from the previous day, the older one, but next to him stood a creature wearing Byron's likeness. In dismay, he looked down at himself and saw not his own tanned and slightly furry chest, but the boney, flat torso of a boy.

"Yesterday's session was to open you up a little, so to speak, and prepare you for further work," said the Devil. He pointed to Byron, and Byron rose to his feet like a marionette. "Today, you get to relive the damage you caused, exactly how it happened."

Fear clawed at Byron's throat, making it hard to breathe. His face hurt, and when he touched it, he felt both the heat of a bruise on his cheek and the wetness of tears.

"What is—" Byron choked out with a sob, a small part of him struggling against the alien feelings that coursed through his mind, causing him to shudder and gasp. *This is not me.* "What is going on?"

"You will experience Sam's fears and his pain, over and over again, until you make them your own," said Lucifer with a small head nod, and the metal collar appeared in his doppelganger's hand. The Sam part of him quailed and blubbered as it was put on him, convinced that he wore death around his neck, while the Byron part of him that knew the collar was harmless could only stand back and watch.

He wanted to turn his head to see Lucifer, but he had no

control over his body. However, when he was turned in place to take position on his knees, the Devil was nowhere to be seen.

"Please, mister," Byron heard himself say in a quavering voice, "I'll suck your cock. I'll let you stick it in me…"

He shook with sobs as the demon wearing his face let out a low, malicious laugh.

LUCIFER SCRUBBED HIS FACE HARD, TIRED OF WEARING THE guise of Michael. Being in close proximity to Byron was frustrating because he was far too observant and the way his questions mirrored his own was irritating. Instead of just thinking himself to his office, he decided to walk to clear his head.

A few levels down from where Byron was being kept, the matter-wrights were busy excavating, creating much needed new space for the ever-expanding population of Hell. Never before in the history of humankind had there been such a steady influx of those needing rehabilitation—Hell was literally bursting at the seams. Lucifer nodded to the foreman, a big Abaddonian who went by the name of Saul, as he walked past. He thought he heard a few whispers from the small, bug-eyed wrights; the Devil hadn't made much of an appearance in the last five centuries, so the sight of him stalking the hallways was causing a bit of a stir. He smiled politely at the huge, ebony-skinned seeder growing the new jail cells when she called out to him:

"Have a good day, sir."

"And you as well."

However, as soon as he was around the corner, he purposefully picked up his step so no one else would try to engage him. Lucifer passed by a cell where he could hear a man screaming but felt no urge to take a peek to see what was happening. Once upon a time, he had delighted in taking part of rehabilitation sessions, the more brutal the better; he'd *lived* for the blood, tears, and screams. These days, he left it all up to the enforcers and reapers and blood-wraiths, preferring to distance himself from it all. Most nights, he just passed off his paperwork to his assistants and then binge watched Netflix for hours on end.

He was in a weird slump.

Lucifer climbed the steps to his office and let himself in. Across the room was a low couch, and he made a beeline for it, bringing into being a cold bottle of beer as he walked. However, after he sat down, he frowned at the beer—a glass of red wine replaced it a second later, and his brow smoothed out. He took a small sip and rolled it over his tongue slowly.

Château Pradeaux 2008. It was, as he'd said to Byron, amazing. With a sigh, he slouched back against the soft red suede carefully so as not to spill wine on himself.

He'd been furious when the council had ordered him to reap Byron's soul himself, but once he was out in the world, pulled away from the seclusion that had turned him into a near recluse, he'd found himself having a good time.

Yes, Byron was a violent, sadistic psychopath who killed for the sheer joy of it but compared to what Lucifer had accomplished over millennia… Well, he was just a novice.

Who am I to judge? Lucifer smiled and closed his eyes.

But, if he was honest with himself, it had been nice to sit there, just two men discussing art, music, literature, science… Byron, despite his murderous shortcomings, was quite the Renaissance man. He also made for a good listener. Lucifer grinned, shaking his head. He'd been equal parts repelled and attracted to Byron. It was a titillating juxtaposition of feelings—the resulting heated passion of the ride back to Byron's manor home and the excitement over his inevitable betrayal had been completely genuine.

Was it all an act? When Byron had asked him the question, he had been forced to lie. Lucifer contemplated his glass again, remembering the way Byron's eyes had brightened with delight at "Michael's" appreciation of the fine wine.

Am I just... lonely? It was ridiculous even to consider, but his laugh came out sounding a little strained. Lucifer replaced the wine with a bottle of beer and shook his head. No, it was his maker meddling about in his affairs, trying to teach him some lesson or another. Why else would xe have barred Lucifer from reading Byron's mind? And making him plan out Byron's sessions himself? What the hell was that about?

Lucifer let out a long sigh at that thought and held out his hand for the folder containing Byron's crimes. It appeared a moment later, but he waited until he'd finished half his beer before opening it. He flipped to one of the earlier records and settled back to read.

MIND OVER MATTER

Lucifer folded his hands in his lap and stared at Byron, a slightly exasperated look on the Devil's handsome face. Things were obviously not going the way he wanted them to, that much was evident.

"You can't just *defy* what's happening to you," Lucifer argued. "It doesn't work that way in Hell. At least it shouldn't."

"But… ?" The chairs that day were overstuffed, plush things in vibrant orange. They were absurdly hideous and extremely comfortable at once.

"Well. See, there should have been some sort of progress so far," replied the Devil. What looked like a sheaf of dot matrix printouts appeared in his hand, and he flipped through a few pages. "But, there's… nothing. Zilch. Nada."

"Ah." Byron felt a small thrill that he was somehow able to exert his will over the process. Did that mean, however, that the efforts of his tormentors would increase? He tried to set aside that worry and concentrated on the man in front of him.

For once, Lucifer wasn't posturing or being flippant. He seemed honestly perplexed. He studied Byron for a moment, and the pages disappeared from his hand.

"You're going to be raped and skinned alive. Repeatedly. Aren't you afraid?"

"Of course I am," said Byron. His heart rate had accelerated with the word *skinned*. His nostrils flared as he took a deep breath to try to calm himself. "Does that mean I can expect Saeed or Thomas?"

Creases appeared on Lucifer's forehead.

"Saeed. But"—he shook his head, his dark eyes shrewd—"how are you *doing* this? You should be beside yourself with terror, pleading with me."

"Like I said before: *mind over matter*. If I am just mind… There is no matter to fear."

"Yes, but you don't seem to understand what I'm getting at. You *are* matter here. This isn't just some hallucination or spirit journey or whatever the fuck you think it is. You *exist* here."

Byron tilted his head, equal parts curious and disturbed by the news.

"How am I matter? Isn't my dead body rotting in the ground somewhere? It has been… what… three weeks now? Four?"

"A little over fifteen minutes."

Stunned, Byron sat forward.

"But—"

"How do you think we have time to process everyone if we keep time with the mortal realm? You think we're swamped now, you should have seen us when we were closer to Earth time," said Lucifer. "The downside to it, however, is that technology is really touch-and-go, which gums up the works and makes everyone cranky, but we come out ahead in the end—though barely."

"So that's the reason behind the printed pages and the intercoms and your Rolodex," said Byron with a little nod.

"Yes… Wait, how did you know I have a Rolodex?"

"Just a guess." Byron allowed himself a grin. It was fascinating but completely outside the limits of his own rather specialized imagination.

Yet he still couldn't commit to the idea that this was *actually* happening to him. "But… Why can't you just, you know"—he gestured to his head vaguely—"keep all that information in memory."

Lucifer burst out laughing.

"Who do you think I am? *God?* That's literally *millions* of names." However, his moment of mirth ended abruptly, and he scowled at Byron. "You know that won't work."

"What won't?"

"This chit-chatty, trying to get to know you better, 'Oh that is *fascinating*, Mr. Satan, sir!' thing you're doing. You can't think that trying to get all buddy-buddy with me is going to make me go soft on you."

"It never occurred to me," lied Byron, reining in his irritation over the caricature Lucifer had just made of him. "And I do hope that's not how it sounds to you."

"Good," said Lucifer, but he sat back in his chair and gestured to Byron. "But… To answer your question: there are tiny pieces of the mortal you inside the form you inhabit here. They contain all the same information you had within you at death, except at a fraction of the density. You're an *F* dimensional copy of yourself until we can get the right energy to start burning away the dark metastasis that is overtaking what you could consider your 'soul.' Once that's complete, through these sessions, you'll be reabsorbed into the Light."

"*F* dimensional?" Byron lifted his eyebrows.

"Yeah. It's like the second dimension but slightly higher." The Devil lifted his hand about a foot from his knee, then turned his palm sideways.

Shaking his head, Byron couldn't help feeling that Lucifer was making fun of him.

"You're inventing all this."

"I'm truly not," replied Lucifer. "But I don't know why I'm bothering to tell you all of this anyway." He glanced at the big analogue watch on his wrist. "Besides, Saeed will be here any minute to start on you."

Panic hit Byron again hard—a shot of adrenaline had his pulse racing so fast that he felt nauseous and lightheaded almost instantly. He took another slow breath. The fact that he actually had substance here didn't change anything, he decided. He would continue trying to keep the fear under control for as long as possible.

A dark shape coalesced across the room. Tall and thickly muscled like a body builder, Saeed stepped out of the shadows. His black hair hung down past his sharp cheekbones, and he stared out at Byron from beneath his dark brows with eyes the colour of amber. Beautiful Saeed.

It was not Saeed however. It was a demon, just like all the others had been. Maybe he was a demon with two cocks to rip him wide. Maybe he had semen so cold that it would freeze Byron's bowels until he felt his tissues shatter. Maybe he was simply strong and could tear his limbs from his body.

The knife in Saeed's hand had a fixed three-and-three-quarter-inch drop-point blade with a razor-sharp guthook, full-length tang, and rosewood grip: a buck-skinning knife. Byron knew it well—after all, his father had given it to him for his sixteenth birthday.

Lucifer slapped his knees.

"Well, I will leave you to your session," he said, rising to his feet.

The seat under Byron winked out of existence, and he landed hard on the smooth floor. He scrambled to his knees. As had happened every time Lucifer went to depart, Byron's fear doubled, then trebled. Had he anything in his system at all, he would have soiled himself in terror.

"Please," he whispered in a panic, his voice rendered as thin as a breath of air. The Devil turned and looked at him, shaking his head.

"Save your begging for *him*," Lucifer said, pointing to the demon wearing Saeed's form. "I have no use for it now. Too little, too late. I'm not going to save you from reliving your crimes just because you ask me nicely."

"Nuh-no," said Byron, shaking pathetically as the huge demon stalked towards him. He had been much more careful with Saeed than he'd been with Thomas. Saeed had lasted far, far longer. He tried to steady his voice. "Just stay. Please stay."

A furrow appeared between the Devil's brows as he appraised Byron.

"Will it lessen your fear?"

In his panic, Byron realized he hadn't thought through his plea. He stared, slack-jawed, at Lucifer, unable to answer. The knife Saeed held touched the side of his throat, and he let out a shaky, hoarse breath.

"That's what I thought," muttered the Devil. However, right before he disappeared, Byron thought he saw a note of uncertainty in those dark eyes.

SAEED IBN MUHAMMAD AL-RABI' – 1976–1998

Saeed tied off the stitch and snipped the end neatly before starting on the next one. The six-inch gash would leave a scar, that was for certain, but the edges were clean, and it sort of followed the curve of the girl's calf. It might not even be that noticeable when it healed.

"Beautiful work, Saeed," said Dr. Danielsen, watching him as he worked. "It doesn't surprise me that you want to be a surgeon. You've got the steadiest hands I've seen in some time."

Grinning to himself, Saeed felt his face get a little flushed at the compliment.

"My mother said that I should have been named Asbat, meaning 'steady' or 'reliable'… though I'm glad I wasn't, considering how most people would pronounce it."

The cheerleader getting the stitches let out giggle, and Saeed smiled wider.

"From what I've seen of you, 'happy' suits you just as well," commented Dr. Danielsen.

Saeed tilted his head in surprise but kept his focus on his work. However, he could see the man supervising him out of the corner of his eye, close enough that he could smell the subtle, expensive cologne he wore.

"You know Arabic?"

"I know a little, yes," replied Dr. Danielsen with a chuckle. "Not much, I'm afraid."

"Well, I think my parents preferred the meaning 'successful,' if I'm honest," said Saeed with a rueful smile.

After knotting the last stitch, he rolled the stool sideways and rooted through the drawer of adhesive bandages and pulled out a few large ones. He quickly covered the gash with one.

"You're done!" he said to the girl. She sat up, her gold curls mussed and cheeks a little pale. The tight V-neck shirt displayed her prominent breasts to advantage, and he wondered idly to himself whether she should be wearing a more substantial bra considering all the hopping and spinning she did. He pulled out his pad and wrote a quick prescription. "Keep your wound dry for a day. No soaking it for at least two. Keep it covered if it's going to get dirty," he said, smiling at the cheerleader. He handed her the scrip and the extra bandages. "I'm prescribing you a mild painkiller for your leg and your shoulder. If the pain in the shoulder persists, come back and we'll take another x-ray, but I think you should be fine."

"Thank you, Doctor," she said with a relieved smile.

"You're welcome. Make an appointment for two weeks from now to get those out, and for goodness sake, be more careful."

Saeed watched her leave and then peeled off his gloves, dumping them with the gauze and needle into the yellow hazardous wastebin. When he finally turned to his supervisor, he saw that Dr. Danielsen was leaning back against the counter with his hands in his pockets and a strange look on his face.

"Pretty girl," said Dr. Danielsen, angling his head at the door. "Wouldn't you say so?"

Saeed blinked and looked in that direction, feeling slightly discomfited.

"Ah... yes," he agreed a little nervously. Had he shown

something of himself in the fact that he hadn't commented first on the girl's... endowments? Despite it being grossly unprofessional, the other male doctors at the hospital tended to make all sorts of observations about their female patients. Saeed normally went along with it though it made him uncomfortable to do so. However, he had not expected that sort of lecherous behaviour from Dr. Byron Danielsen. "Very hot... legs," he finished lamely.

To his surprise, Dr. Danielsen laughed, his pale-blue eyes crinkled at the corners with his mirth. The older doctor was handsome, like an actor in a movie, and he was always charming. Saeed didn't understand why some people called Dr. Danielsen strange—he seemed like a really nice guy.

"I apologize," said Dr. Danielsen with a friendly smile. "That was my rather roundabout, backwards way of trying to assess where your... ah... *interests* lay." He pushed himself away from the counter to step closer to Saeed.

Stunned, Saeed stood up quickly, sending the stool rolling slowly across the room.

"I'm sorry?"

"You didn't react at all when the girl was obviously flirting with you. I assumed..."

Flirting? How did I miss that?

"You assumed wrong, Doctor Danielsen. I don't understand how it's any of your business. Perhaps I was just being professional, did that not occur to you?" Then Saeed realized that he was probably overreacting and shrugged his shoulders. "I'm sorry for raising my voice, but what I do on my own time is private and please respect that."

Dr. Danielsen pulled his hands out of his pockets to hold them up in a gesture of supplication.

"Saeed, if I crossed a line or assumed wrongly, I am very sorry. I took a chance," he said, his expression sheepish. "It's just... Well, seeing as I'm leaving the hospital in two weeks, and we'll no longer be colleagues, I was hoping that you and I might have dinner at some point. But it seems I was wrong. Again, I'm sorry."

Saeed just stared mutely as Dr. Danielsen turned and walked out of the room. It took a few seconds for him to realize that his legs were shaking and his pulse was erratic. He sat down on the corner of the exam table, filled with a mixture of shock and excitement.

The prudent thing to do, of course, was to avoid Dr. Danielsen whenever he could. However, as Saeed was standing by the sink a few minutes later, soaping the smell of latex off his hands, he was replaying the conversation in his head and giving it a much different ending:

"Yes, Doctor Danielsen, I would very much enjoy having supper with you... to get to know one another better..."

DESPITE THE RUMOURS THAT DR. DANIELSEN WAS LEAVING because he had lost his license, the hospital was throwing him a big goodbye party. As Saeed lingered near the table with the cake, he listened to a couple of radiology techs discussing the doctor's departure.

"I hear his father donated a cool million to St. Mary's to cover it up," said the blond with the unfortunate raspberry mark down the side of her face.

"Really?" said the brunette. She took a sip from her plastic wineglass and looked over at Dr. Danielsen who was standing surrounded by a group of doctors and nurses. "Where did you hear that?"

"I overheard Doctor Townsend and Doctor Singh talking about it in the break room a few weeks ago."

"Really?" asked the brunette again. "Did you hear what happened?"

Under the guise of getting more punch, Saeed moved a little

closer so he could hear better. However, the girls noticed him and shone wide smiles in his direction.

"Oh, hi," said the blond. "Doctor al-Rabi', is it?"

"Yes. But, please, call me Saeed," he replied. He took a sip from the Styrofoam cup and smiled awkwardly at the two women.

"I thought Muslims didn't drink," said the brunette, whose name might have been Lydia.

"Who said I was Muslim?" said Saeed with a little shrug. Across the room, Dr. Byron Danielsen lifted his head and looked around, searching for someone. When his eyes alighted on Saeed, his face broke into a smile and Saeed's pulse kicked up in response.

An hour later, Saeed stood in the rain, clutching the address to Dr. Danielsen's brownstone in his fist. When the party had become more raucous due to some of the staff having partaken in too much of the free liquor, Saeed had found himself sequestered in one of the small offices in the out-patient clinic with Dr. Danielsen and Dr. Goldberg, discussing the changeover of his supervision. The lights had been low, and despite the presence of the rather portly head of surgery, it had felt strangely intimate.

For the past two weeks, Saeed had thought about what Dr. Danielsen had said to him. He'd agonized over whether he'd been mistaken in assuming that Dr. Danielsen had meant a date. Maybe it had been merely an invitation to supper without the potential of something more? However, the attraction he'd seen in the older man's eyes when he'd looked over Dr. Goldberg's head at him was blatant.

Saeed found it hard to breathe, staring up at the doctor's home. He'd never been with a man, despite the fact that it was a desire that felt all consuming at times, driving him to push his body to its utmost limits to escape it. It was bad enough that his parents proclaimed their displeasure at his unmarried state every chance they got; if his family found out he was a homosexual, they would disown him.

Yet, when the meeting had finished and Dr. Danielsen had secretly pressed a small card into his grasp when they shook hands before parting ways, Saeed had been nearly beside himself with excitement. He'd retreated to the locker room in haste, and only when he was completely certain that he was alone did he take a look at the card in his hand. Written on the back of the doctor's business card in a graceful script was an address and the words:

Late supper? Please come, Saeed. 9pm. Saeed had sat in the harshly lit room for nearly twenty minutes trying to talk himself out of going.

With a deep breath, Saeed steadied himself and pressed the doorbell. After a moment, the thick door opened.

"I'm so glad you decided to join me," said the older man with a smile.

"I was glad for the invitation, Doctor Danielsen," replied Saeed, amazed at how steady his voice was.

"Please... Call me Byron."

SAEED ARCHED HIS BACK, EMBARRASSED BY HOW HARD HE WAS panting but he was unable to stop himself. It felt so good to be touched this way. Caressed. Teased.

"Come, make a little noise for me, beautiful Saeed," whispered Byron against the side of his neck. His hand slid slowly down Saeed's shaft and squeezed. "I want to hear your pleasure."

Saeed let out a flustered laugh. Hear his pleasure? He shook his head.

"I don't know how."

"Yes, you do. I won't let you climax until you show me."

Face scorching, Saeed blinked back the shameful tears in his eyes. He wasn't lying. He had no idea what Byron wanted to hear. He thought about the pornographic movies he had watched, first with women—there was *no* way he could go on like they did—then with men. The men had been quieter, but that somehow had made it more intense for Saeed as he had furtively stroked himself in the little theatre.

The hand slid back up his erection and lingered, teasing only gently at the engorged head until Saeed finally let out a tiny moan.

"Beautiful," Byron murmured. "Again… a little louder. Show me that you love being touched."

Saeed nearly shook his head again, but then Byron quickly rose up on his knees and bowed down over Saeed's waist. When his tongue touched the very tip of Saeed's erection—right against the slit, warm and wet—the sound that came from Saeed's mouth was very much like an animal's noise. Byron pulled away with a chuckle.

"Yes, just like that Saeed. Let me hear it. Let me hear how it feels when a man licks your cock. Show me how you love it, and I'll make you cum."

He exhaled sharply and panted a few breaths, then let out a low moan when Byron enveloped him in his hot mouth again. The very fact that the doctor had used dirty language ramped up Saeed's fervour. A full-throated groan burst out of him when Byron began to move faster, licking and sucking, and fondling his testicles with one hand while the other stroked him with the same rhythm of his mouth. Eyes squeezed shut, he whimpered and moaned as Byron brought him closer and closer to orgasm.

"Beautiful Saeed," said Byron, drawing back for a moment, his lips wet and eyes wide. "Would you like to cum in my mouth?"

Without any need for prompting, Saeed made a strangled noise and replied: "Oh yes, Doctor Danielsen. Please, yes…" He felt little shame at the words, so lost as he was in the moment. Then, when the older man began to work at him again with skilled hands and mouth, Saeed's noises grew louder. Finally, he climaxed with a gasp, his whole body twitching in time to the glorious pulses of pleasure that erupted from deep inside him as Byron milked and stroked him with tongue and lips.

Breathing heavily, he groaned, and another little shudder went through him before he lay still. He was sensitive, so very sensitive, and the slow, deliberate lapping of his glans was almost too much. However, Byron stopped and stretched out next to Saeed with a smile on his face.

"I take it that you found that pleasant?" Byron chuckled at Saeed's dazed nod. "I haven't done that since Michael…" The doctor's smile faded and Saeed felt a touch of worry. However, Byron just shook his head as if confused. Then, he stroked down Saeed's furry chest and traced over his thick muscles with a finger. "You have quite the physique, my boy. Seems like you've been putting your pent-up energy to good use at least. I still can't believe you've waited so long to let a man get his hands on you."

Saeed grinned a little sheepishly, and he felt some heat in his face, but in the afterglow everything seemed easier.

"I've never really been approached before."

"No? I find that surprising. You're exceedingly beautiful."

Byron's words made him feel shy but wonderful, and he put away his worries for the future to concentrate on the moment instead. Saeed tentatively reached for the doctor, but Byron just chuckled again and gently pushed his hand away.

"Not yet," he said, tweaking one of Saeed's nipples in a playful way. "I have something I have to do for a bit. Why don't you sleep some? I'll wake you when I'm done."

Feeling the tiniest bit relieved that he wouldn't have to test his amateur skills just yet, Saeed just nodded. He was tired after all…

SAEED WOKE UP TO A SHOCKING, ACRID SMELL THAT BURNED his nostrils. In complete confusion he stared wide-eyed at the face that peered into his. It was covered in a surgical mask, but he recognized Byron's clear blue eyes.

"Wha…" he tried, but his thoughts were bouncing around in his skull, unable to settle on a word. It took him a second to realize that his arms were bound above his head, and that he stood naked in the middle of a dark stone room that looked like a basement. Saeed was cold, disoriented, and had a horrible taste in his mouth as if he'd been sick. Byron nodded at him as if satisfied that he was awake and placed the bottle of smelling salts on the little table in front of Saeed.

"Doctor Danielsen?" Saeed blinked hard a few times, trying to clear the fog from his eyes. "What are you doing?"

"I so enjoyed hearing your pleasure, Saeed. Truly that was a gift, and I thank you. Now you're going to give me another gift. This time I would like to hear your pain." Byron lifted a scalpel off the small metal table.

Terror squeezed out all thoughts except those of escape, and Saeed tried to kick out. However, his ankles were also tied, and he couldn't even pull them together. Before he had a chance to say anything else, Dr. Danielsen grabbed Saeed's left nipple between finger and thumb, stretched it out, and then quickly sliced it off. Saeed screamed in agony and again when Dr. Danielsen did the same with his right nipple.

The pain was horrific, and he twitched and shuddered as he cried out in fear and anguish.

"Why—" His word ended in another scream as the scalpel slid down from his suprasternal notch to his mons pubis in one quick strike. Blood poured down his legs and his bladder gave out, adding to the mess. Nearly blind with pain, he watched the doctor fill a syringe with something and then inject him with it. Almost instantly, he felt his heart slow, causing him to feel lightheaded and nauseous. Dr. Danielsen smeared something over his chest, frowning as he worked.

"With the application of chitosan and other topical hemostats, as well as the careful use of a cocktail of antifibrinolytic and beta-blockers, I think I can keep you alive long enough to skin you completely," he said quietly. Saeed stared, agape, just a choking sound coming from his throat as his senses began to shut down. "The trick to it though, is not so much keeping you from bleeding out. That I can control. It's the shock that got Thomas in the end. Shame, really."

The scalpel worked around Saeed's shoulder, and when Dr. Danielsen pushed his fingers under the skin and began to wrench it off like a sleeve, Saeed passed out.

SAEED AWOKE TO MORE PAIN, BUT IT WAS DULLED AND FAR away. He groggily looked around, and then down at his chest. He could see muscles where Dr. Danielsen had cut away a huge swath of skin. Over it was a membrane of what looked like clear plastic, and Saeed wondered vaguely if it was keeping him alive. Could one really survive being skinned?

Out of the corner of his eye, he saw someone approaching, but he could only stare mutely. Dr. Danielsen was naked and covered in blood, and with horror, Saeed saw that his penis was erect. What kind of monster was this? Music played from a small radio set on the concrete floor, covered in more plastic sheeting to shield it from blood. It was Beethoven, Saeed thought. He could barely keep his eyes open, and his mind felt like it was drifting. He was fading again.

Dr. Danielsen circled behind him and smeared something cold on his anus. Saeed weakly shook his head.

"Nuhh…" His voice was barely a whisper, scrubbed of any substance by the endless screams.

When the doctor pushed himself into Saeed and began to fuck him with long thrusts, the pain was nothing—

Lucifer curled his lip, disgusted by what he was reading. Byron was completely and utterly depraved. However, he was even more disgusted with himself for how fucking hard he was after reading about Byron's grisly hobby. Lucifer let out a huff of breath and squeezed himself through his pants. Teeth gritted, he closed his eyes and leaned back in the chair.

You can't. You won't.

Lucifer didn't know what had changed. He'd never so much as batted an eye about rubbing one out over someone's rap sheet, and here he was, with a sick feeling in the pit of his stomach. Then his brow furrowed as he remembered something. He stopped fondling himself and flipped back a few pages.

"I haven't done that since Michael…"

GETTING TO THE MEAT

Byron woke up with his head in someone's lap. It was a woman. He could tell because as she stroked his hair, she hummed to herself softly. Shifting slightly, he stared up into Gloria's concerned face. She shook her head a little, and her full lips made a moue of sadness.

"You poor thing," she said quietly. Her fingernails scratched lightly at his scalp, and it sent shivers down his back. He couldn't understand how she could be there, sitting cross-legged in his tiny smooth-walled cell. "Poor, poor thing." She smiled at him, as kind as a mother.

"How are you here?" he asked.

"I'm always here with you," she replied. Her stroking fingers were soothing, and Byron decided then that he didn't care whether she was a hallucination or not. It was nice to see her.

"I don't know how much of this I can take," he admitted.

"You can take far more than what they've done to you," replied Gloria. "You're strong, Mr. Danielsen. Very strong."

Byron closed his eyes and just breathed slowly, letting himself fall into the fantasy and relax. The perfect assistant, always in her immaculate suits and makeup, seeing to his every wish… Of course, she would have followed him to Hell.

"I think you're right about Lucifer, you know," she said in her husky voice.

"Hm?"

"I think he's lost his nerve."

"Really?" Byron felt drained after his encounter with Saeed. He was already starting to drift off again, building up his strength to survive the next horror the Devil would put him through. He idly wondered when they would get to the Richardsons and whether he would have his own dismembered cock shoved up his ass. He very nearly laughed even though the idea nauseated him.

"Really. What other reason could he have for not wanting to take part in the sessions? He certainly gets his back up every time you ask him… and that look in his eye, almost like he's afraid," said Gloria.

"Hm?" He was too worn out for a proper conversation, but he liked the sound of Gloria's voice. "Afraid?"

"Maybe just a little. Maybe he's worried that you'll find out that he's lost the taste for torture. Do you think he's gone soft?"

Byron shrugged, and then he must have fallen asleep because the next time he opened his eyes, he was alone again. He slowly sat up, thinking about what Gloria had said about Lucifer having gone soft. Byron had already tried to get a rise out of his jailer before, to no avail. Was it worth another try just to glean more information out of him? To maybe figure out a way of getting free?

One thing was for certain: Byron really had nothing to lose, did he?

WHEN LUCIFER SHOWED UP A SHORT WHILE LATER, DRESSED in a natty white linen suit and a Panama hat at a rakish angle, Byron greeted him with a sneer. Lucifer's brows rose high on his forehead as he sat down on the green velvet, antique wingback he had conjured for that day.

"I wish I knew how you were doing this," Lucifer said after a moment, gesturing at Byron in a helpless fashion. "It makes no fucking sense. I should see remorse in your eyes, not *contempt* for Christ's sake."

"Maybe you're doing this wrong. You seem out of practice," replied Byron from where he remained standing.

"Wrong? No. I may be out of practice, but I'm following standard protocol." A plasticized paper appeared in Lucifer's hand, and he pointed to it. "It's not rocket science."

"How do you know that your minions are handling me correctly if you're too afraid to stay and watch?"

"Excuse me?"

Byron lifted his chin a touch, staring down at his nose at the Devil.

"I think you've gone soft. You obviously can't stomach watching them torture me," he said with a smirk. "Do you know how *ridiculous* that makes you? You're weak. *Pathetic.*" He made his voice heavy with scorn even though his heart had begun to beat harder—the red mist that surrounded Lucifer was brighter and *pulsed* in the air. Lucifer stared up at Byron, his dark eyes unreadable. "You should be *revelling* in my torture. Glorying in my pain and suffering. *You* should be the one raping me until my screams…"—Byron kept himself from taking a step back when Lucifer lurched to his feet, coming close enough that their noses nearly touched—"until my screams drown in blood. Instead you disappear, pointed tail tucked between your legs like the worm you are."

"You think *that's* why I leave?" Lucifer's voice was dangerously low, his breath hot against Byron's lips. "You think I don't want to tear you apart and bathe in your blood? Drink in your pain? Ohhh, little mortal, how mistaken you are."

The red mist stung Byron's skin as it surrounded him, and he wondered if he had just made an incredible blunder. When he tried to move, he discovered he couldn't. Lucifer let out a soft laugh and stroked his hands down Byron's chest. They were so hot they nearly burned, but the pain was nothing compared to the agony he felt when Lucifer's fingers encircled his cock and squeezed. The heat was terrible, and Byron smelled burned hair and flesh as his blood boiled, his mind sharpening to a razor point of focus. His whole world was pain.

"Did it not occur to you that your pathetic, weak mind could not take what I would do to you? That one measly little man does nothing but whet my appetite? I am the Lord of Hell, you craven maggot. It takes a *legion* to feed my desires!" Lucifer growled his words, his teeth bared and eyes held impossibly wide. He lifted his hand and showed Byron the remains of his penis—a charred, black nugget in his palm. "My cock has bloodied billions, you mewling pustule." He closed his fist and ashes fell from it.

It was relentless, all-consuming agony. Nothing existed for Byron but naked, mind-searing pain he couldn't escape from. When he was finally released from his stasis, the shrieks that poured unending from his raw throat filled him with an even greater terror.

He was powerless to stop Lucifer when he conjured a huge blade and began to butcher him like an animal. Every little cut was amplified, magnified, and rendered utterly *profound*. There was no corner for his mind to escape to, no way to shield himself from any of it. Instead of eventually succumbing to the anguish and sinking into a cool, insensate darkness like he had with the others, he was kept conscious by Lucifer. There was no respite for Byron.

Again and again, Lucifer took him to pieces—the Devil's blade separated joints, severed tendons, dug into his viscera, turned him into meat. Then he would laugh, and Byron would find himself whole, made to suffer anew.

Hours or days, Byron had no concept of how long it went on,

only that the sustained terror and torture were the beginning and end of his existence.

Then finally, once Lucifer had finished raping Byron's limbless, bloodied torso with a monstrous cock that tore him wide open, the Devil tossed him to the ground with a scowl. Panting, he stood over Byron and wiped his mouth on his forearm. Byron stared, unable to blink with lidless eyes, and waited for Lucifer to start over with him.

"*Huhleeze…*" he whispered, teeth naked of lips. "*Huhleeze.*"

"Please? *Please?* You've think you've had enough?" shouted Lucifer.

"*No…*" Byron's voice was a mere hiss. "Ahh… again. *Huhleeze.*"

The Devil blinked, startled. Then he shook his head.

"Oh, fuck *off.*"

Lucifer gestured, and Byron's consciousness winked out.

Straight Out of Hell

When Byron opened his eyes, he was free of pain, whole in body, and on his back on the warm floor of his cell. He lay there for a moment, feeling a little odd, and as he rubbed his face, he tried to figure out what had changed. Maybe the pain inflicted by Lucifer had been so complete that without it, he was empty in comparison. Frowning, he thought about how strange it was that, by the end of their "session," he had craved the shrieking crescendo of anguish… It had become *divine*.

He heard a noise and turned his head. Lying a few feet away, also on his back and staring at the ceiling, was Lucifer. The Devil was covered head-to-toe in blood, and the butcher knife rested on his naked chest—Byron watched it rise and fall with his breathing.

After a moment, Lucifer sighed and shook his head.

"You were right," he said in a bone-weary tone. "You were fucking *right*."

Byron sat up slowly, his brow furrowed. Lucifer turned to look at him, his expression skirting the line between bitter and amused.

"Right about what?" asked Byron.

Lucifer smiled crookedly. "I don't have the stones to do this any more. I've gone *soft*, as you put it."

Head tilted, Byron stared at him for a beat.

"But… You're so *good* at it," he ventured.

Brows high, Lucifer's grin widened for a moment. "I am, aren't I?" he said with a chuckle, but then he just sighed again and looked back up at the ceiling. "I *used* to enjoy it."

"You didn't this time?" Byron felt strangely disappointed when the corners of Lucifer's mouth turned down, and he shook his head in reply. "You seemed like you were…"

"I really had to push myself there at the end of it," confessed Lucifer. "Truth be told, I haven't enjoyed torturing anyone for a very long time. Hell, I don't even seem to get off on it unless it's on paper… And even then, I feel like shit afterwards for doing it."

"Oh." Byron didn't know what to say. However, before the silence became uncomfortable, Lucifer sat up and gave him a look that bordered on the mischievous.

"Hey, let's get out of here," said the Devil, brushing some of the dried blood from his arms and chest. The knife had disappeared.

Byron frowned. "What do you mean? Out of Hell?"

"Sure. Obviously you're immune to rehabilitation. There's really nothing more I can do, so I give up," replied Lucifer with a shrug. He stood and held out his hand. "Fuck it, right? Let's go grab a bite to eat somewhere. People watch a little. Shoot the shit. I don't care… Fuck the rules."

With a laugh, Byron accepted Lucifer's help and got to his feet.

"All right. Won't your god stop us?"

"It's not as if xe's answered any of my questions lately," replied Lucifer with his lip curled. "Let's go. I'm sick to death of this place."

"Ok. Where are we going?"

"I know a great little spot in Madrid, right in the Plaza Mayor. It's a little touristy, but they make some of the best *Salmorejo* I've ever had, and their wine list is good. Well, not *Clin d'Oeil* good, but… You game?"

Byron shook his head in amusement, his grin wide.

"I am," he replied. "Lead the way."

. . .

FANNING HIMSELF WITH THE TAPAS MENU, BYRON SQUINTED across the square, watching the throng of tourists milling around the base of the equestrian statue of Philip III. Across the table, Lucifer was ordering for both of them in rapid-fire Spanish that Byron couldn't follow. It was hot, nearly unbearably so, but Byron would have put up with far worse just to be out of his cell and away from its denizens.

Well, with the exception of the Lord of Hell, I suppose.

He turned to Lucifer and saw that the handsome young man was smiling at him. They were both dressed in light-coloured slacks and short-sleeved shirts, but Lucifer had on a straw-coloured fedora as well. He looked completely at ease—the stiffness and mocking arrogance he normally displayed was gone for the moment. Byron picked a spiced olive out of the little brown ceramic bowl and chewed it thoughtfully.

"So does this mean I can start calling you Luce?" he asked, cocking an eyebrow.

"What? Oh. No… We're not friends. Not by a long shot. This is just a break," replied Lucifer. The waiter returned, and they watched him uncork the bottle of the *Rioja* they'd ordered and toss the wrapper from the neck of it over his shoulder before setting down the bottle in the middle of the table and walking away.

Byron laughed, thinking about how proper Angélique was in comparison, and Lucifer joined in, his thoughts obviously running parallel. Though not friends, they certainly weren't enemies, and Byron decided he was happy about that.

"So," he said. "Does the existence of Hell mean that the Christians were right? There's only one god and everyone, religion be damned, has to go through the same process."

Lucifer swallowed his mouthful and shook his head. The red mist around him swirled with the motion, invisible to everyone but Byron and himself.

"Oh, not at all. Christianity actually has nothing to do with it. Well, not *nothing*," he answered, after taking a sip of wine. "We've obviously borrowed motifs from them—from mortals in general, actually. Hell's changed a lot through the ages, and it's humans who are responsible. It's not even really called *Hell*. It has no fixed name, and it encompasses all religions and beliefs in the shape it takes."

"Even religions that don't believe in any form of punishment or, as you like to put it, *rehabilitation*?"

"Yup. It's complicated, but it works. You, for instance, may claim to have no real religious affiliation, but obviously, you do or else it would have wound up looking different."

"And the one you refer to as your maker. Your god... what about, uh... *xem*? You called xem 'the Almighty,' when we first met. That sounds rather Christian to me," Byron pointed out.

"Nah, that's just a little joke. My maker sits on the council and is responsible for me because xe is *literally* my maker."

"Council? Of how many?" Byron was intrigued by the conversation and thankful that Lucifer was no longer evading his questions.

"More than the number of sand particles on every beach in the world," laughed the Devil. "Countless. There is no number. It's hard to really explain because things work differently there."

"In the *F* dimension?"

"Ha! I'm impressed you remembered that. Yes. It's an overlapping dimension. Things like time, matter, space... It follows different rules."

"So what are you? *F* dimensional beings?" asked Byron. He frowned. "Aliens?"

"You could say that," said Lucifer with a nod. He refilled Byron's glass and sat back, his dark eyes amused.

"And you've been around how long?"

"Forever."

"Since the beginning of time?"

"Since the very beginning and the very end of everything."

"Oh," said Byron, trying to wrap his mind around it all. "But… If Hell, or whatever non-name it goes by, is for rehabilitating human beings, how did it come about at the beginning if there were no humans?"

"It was created some time after you all achieved a level of self-awareness above anything that came before," explained Lucifer, gesturing vaguely at Byron with his spoon. "Humans. With your taste for fratricide, you were making a real mess of things."

"Right. But… Why would god, or this council, permit things like murder to begin with? Look at me, for instance. I killed many people, and it took until now for my 'soul' to be reaped, as you put it."

"Yeah. Well… Thing is, the council doesn't actually care anything about human lives."

"They don't? So, it's perfectly fine for people to murder each other? Why the need for Hell then?" Byron wondered what the Christians would think of a god who didn't care one whit for them.

"They only care that the energy gets processed, and that the system continues to work. In fact, psychos like you are sort of good for business because you kill so many innocent people—folks that are relatively unburdened by darkness. Their journey through Hell is as quick as a stamp on a passport. It's the ones that have to go through rehabilitation that are the problem. Not sure what to do about it… I've tried some different approaches but… Well, you saw what it's like."

"Ok. But… If you don't mind me asking, what did *you* do to wind up as the king of it?"

Lucifer frowned.

"Well. It was sort of my idea to begin with. My maker agreed with my plan, and the council voted it into existence. I thought it was because I was respected. Turns out that they saw it as a way of controlling me and limiting my influence in the mortal realm. They didn't like the way I was… *encouraging* certain practices."

"If you hate it so much, can't you ask to leave?"

"I never said I *hated* it, but… Leaving's not that easy."

"So, you're stuck for eternity doing a job that you rather dislike?"

Dark brows low over his eyes, Lucifer's expression took on a touch of annoyance.

"Will you drop it?" he growled.

As Byron tried to think of something else to say, he noticed a tall woman watching him from across the narrow alleyway where he and Lucifer were seated for lunch. She smiled at him.

"Seduce him," mouthed Gloria.

Byron's eyes darted to Lucifer, but he was scowling into his glass of wine. He looked for Gloria but she was gone. Hallucination or not, why would she want him to seduce the Devil? He stared at Lucifer, wondering what he should do.

"Why am I here?" he finally asked.

Lucifer lifted his gaze. "What do you mean?"

"I mean… You could have just left me locked up in my cell and come here by yourself. I'm just curious as to why you brought me here," said Byron.

After blowing out a little air through his lips, his brow wrinkled up, Lucifer shrugged.

"I don't like eating alone?" he offered. "You're moderately interesting to talk to? Listen, I don't know. Don't read too much into it, ok?"

"Ok," replied Byron with a smile. "I'm sorry. I was just thinking that I was enjoying the conversation and was wondering what you were getting out of it." It was said as plainly as possible—he didn't want to be too obvious in his praise—but Lucifer stared at him suspiciously for a moment before answering.

"Well… For one, I'm still intrigued by the mystery of Michael," said Lucifer.

"Michael?"

"Yeah." Lucifer gestured to his bearded face and his brows quirked up. "This is Michael."

"I don't know any Michael," protested Byron, but he felt slightly odd saying it, as if it were a lie.

"So you claim."

"And… for two?"

"Pardon?"

"You said that Michael, whomever he may be, was one reason," said Byron, dipping his bread in the cold tomato soup they had come for. "It just sounded like there was a follow up."

Lucifer snorted and shook his head, and then one cheek dimpled up in a smile.

"You think I actually *like* you," he replied.

"I think you might," said Byron with a little shrug of his own. "I also think that you lied to me when you said that our date was all an act."

"You do, do you?" However, instead of annoyed, Lucifer just seemed amused.

"I do. I think you were honestly enjoying yourself, and judging by this little vacation we're taking together, you want to enjoy yourself again. In my company."

Lucifer looked away, but his smile remained coy.

"Eat your soup," he said.

"What's more, I think you're hoping that I kiss that gorgeous mouth of yours again," murmured Byron, leaning forward. Lucifer's eyes widened, and he stared at Byron for a moment.

"You're flirting with me, and it's not going to work—whatever it is you have planned," he said, and then repeated, "Eat your soup." However, when he went back to his own meal, the swirling red haze that mirrored his actions seemed to be moving faster, as if he was agitated.

Byron smiled.

COME AS YOU ARE

Lucifer unlocked the door and held it open. After Byron stepped past him to enter the space beyond, he laughed softly.

"What's so funny?" asked Lucifer. He locked the door behind him and joined Byron in the small living room of the one-bedroom apartment. Apart from the big, overstuffed brown couch and the unit that held his massive TV and cable modem, the place was empty. His shoes echoing loud on the parquet floors, Byron peeked into the bedroom, and shook his head.

"You don't even have a bed?" asked Byron with obvious amusement.

"Who needs a bed when I have a couch," replied Lucifer. "But… if you want…" He flicked his fingers, borrowing the entire contents of an empty deluxe room at The Plaza in New York City, and filled the bedroom with the hotel's signature red, gold, and ivory furnishings. The king-size bed looked ludicrous in the space, but when Byron chuckled, it held a note of appreciation.

Lucifer sat down on the edge of the couch and watched his guest. The rest of lunch had passed… strangely. It was as if Byron was doing his damnedest to endear himself, and though Lucifer knew there had to be an ulterior motive for the sudden change in tack, he couldn't help be somewhat charmed by the attention. Even if the flirtation was just a psychopath's attempt at manipulation, it was stroking an ego that desperately needed to be stroked. Lucifer chewed on the corner of his lip a moment and frowned warily at Byron as he approached.

"So you weren't making things up when you told me that you had a small apartment in the Heights?" asked the tall blond man with a grin.

Lucifer shook his head.

"But, why? What do you do here?"

"Well… Like I told you, technology in Hell is problematic," said Lucifer, looking over at the big flat-screen.

"So you come here to watch TV?"

"Yeah. I like HBO."

Byron began to laugh again and shook his head, clear blue eyes narrowed at Lucifer.

"You know how ludicrous that sounds?"

"Yes, I do. But"—Lucifer sighed and gestured feebly, trying to convey the depths of his weariness—"I really need to get away sometimes."

"So, you just sit here," said Byron, pointing to the couch, "and spend hours just watching movies?"

Lucifer nodded.

Byron took another step towards Lucifer, his expression thoughtful. "You know, if you were human, I would say that you were depressed."

Lucifer snorted in derision, though it had already occurred to him.

"Now you're the one who sounds ludicrous," he said with a scowl, staring up at Byron. Suddenly, it dawned on him that the crow's-feet at the corners of Byron's eyes weren't as pronounced as they had been before. In fact, his face seemed smoother, the muscles more taut, hair more gold than silver. At the time of death, Byron had been just shy of fifty-two years old. The man standing in front of Lucifer was no older than thirty. Confused, Lucifer stood and grabbed Byron's head, holding him immobile as he stared hard into his eyes. Byron didn't resist and held Lucifer's gaze.

"I don't understand this," muttered Lucifer, realizing the process must have been very gradual for him not to notice. "How is it that you look *younger*?" Most mortals became wasted, ragged versions of themselves after a few sessions. Byron had had dozens, and here he looked better than he had in life. It made no sense.

"I feel different too," replied Byron. "Lighter. Unburdened." He smiled. "Especially after being with you."

Though he was speaking of being tortured beyond what the mortal mind could generally take, his tone was low and tender, like that of a lover's. It was as if what they had shared was not wrought of blood and pain, but something sweet and profound. Lucifer tilted his head, suspicious, but despite himself, felt a *pull*. There was something in Byron's expression that warmed him—made him think how nice it would be to just let go with someone. Someone who knew exactly who he was and what he was capable of.

He tightened his grip on Byron's head a little and got a satisfying wince in return. However, when Lucifer leaned in to bring his mouth close, Byron surprised him by eagerly taking him by the waist to bring their hips flush. The move caused him to loosen his hold enough that Byron sealed the gap and kissed him full on the lips.

It was all an act—Lucifer was absolutely certain. But it didn't keep him from kissing back. He broke away a moment later and glared at Byron, his jaw tight and nostrils flared.

"I don't know what you think you're up to," he said, "but you're under my power here. There is nothing you can do to escape me. You gain *nothing* from this."

Byron nodded, and Lucifer's frown deepened.

"No, I do know that," said Byron. His eyes held no real warmth in them, but his hands crept up under Lucifer's shirt and stroked his sides in a soft way that made the Devil shiver. "Question is, do you want me?"

Lucifer did. He wanted Byron. Even if it was manufactured interest on Byron's part, he realized he craved the contact. He felt a stirring that, for once, was not hounded by disgust. Lucifer let out a gruff noise when Byron found his nipple and rubbed it gently. It hardened under his touch, a sensitive, direct line to his cock. He closed his eyes, breathing heavily through his nose, his resistance melting away under Byron's slow caresses.

What did it matter, really, if he let this happen?

"I know this is a performance," he said in a low voice. "Why are you offering yourself up if you know there is nothing to be gained?"

Byron pulled away.

"I don't know," he confessed. He seemed so completely genuine that it gave Lucifer pause.

"But still, you're going to let me fuck you," said Lucifer, eliminating his clothes with a thought. He stepped back to let Byron see him, his huge cock erect and jutting stiffly upwards. It seemed that Byron's eyes widened a touch at the sight, but he reached out for him nonetheless. His hand was cool on Lucifer's dick as he stroked along his thick shaft, unable to span it completely with finger and thumb.

"Yes. I am," said Byron, his gaze lowered. "You want me; therefore, you can have me." Maybe it was the angle of the light streaming in through the bare windows, but he seemed even younger than before.

Who are you? The tiny bit of hoarseness in Byron's voice spoke more of desire than it did fear. Lucifer swept his hand across Byron's body, rendering him instantly naked, and saw that his long cock was hard as well. Lucifer pulled away and gestured with the knife that had appeared in his grip, pointing it at Byron's groin.

"What if I said I was going to cut your cock off first?" he asked. "That I want you *screaming* as I fuck you?"

Byron's placid, ice-blue eyes met his. Lucifer watched a muscle twitch in his jaw, but he just nodded once. That was all it took.

Lucifer's blade severed Byron's cock from his body in one easy slash, ridding him of his most treasured weapon. The man collapsed on the floor with a high-pitched scream and clutched at his groin, curling in on himself. The pool of blood beneath him spread quickly, leaking out in bright runnels between his fingers. Byron's face was ashen, and when he opened his eyes, the blue of his irises was almost preternaturally bright compared to the broken blood vessels surrounding them.

The display was only marginally arousing. Lucifer frowned and squatted down next to Byron to watch him writhe for a moment longer, the tendons in his neck rigid and his teeth bared in a rictus of pain.

"Is this what you want?" he asked, honestly curious. It seemed that Byron was genuine about offering himself up. What man would agree to have his dick cut off? Byron hadn't even flinched.

"I... *hhhu*... I wuh-want what you... *huhhh* want," panted Byron through his clenched teeth. Tears of agony pooled in his eyes and spilled over.

The point was made.

Lucifer touched Byron lightly and his body sagged immediately. Free of pain, Byron blinked his wet eyes a few times, breathing heavily as he lay still. When he finally pulled his hands away from his crotch, he made a soft sound of bewilderment and sat up. Instead of restoring what he had cut away, Lucifer had simply healed him. Byron stared down at himself—he was as sexless as a doll. However, when he looked back up at Lucifer, he seemed unconcerned by the loss of his cock.

"Fine. Yes, I do want you," conceded Lucifer when the silence grew heavy between them. "It's just that I don't want..."

"What?" Byron's voice was hoarse, and he didn't resist when

Lucifer reached out to take a handful of hair to pull his head back, baring his throat.

"I don't want a struggle," the Devil said quietly.

When Byron answered simply by closing his eyes, Lucifer smiled. He easily manoeuvred the unresisting Byron into position on his hands and knees and took his own cock in hand. Stroking himself rapidly, Lucifer knelt between Byron's calves and slid his thumb over the blush-pink pucker that was presented to him, barely darker than the skin around it and furred lightly with blond hair. Byron was obviously surprised when Lucifer's light touch filled him with lube—he let out a small noise and shifted his hips at the sudden sensation. Though Byron would probably end up tearing, blood made for poor lubricant, and Lucifer simply didn't want to chafe... It had nothing to do with making things easier for Byron. Or so he told himself.

Lucifer moved forward and pushed the huge head of his cock against Byron. In response, Byron went down on his elbows to brace himself. Head to the ground, he locked his fingers behind his head and breathed slowly.

Pumping his hips, Lucifer began trying to force himself into Byron's body. Finally when his sphincter gave and Lucifer's cockhead penetrated the constricting opening, Byron let out a loud, pain-filled cry. The Devil paused, his own breathing a tad unsteady, and he smiled when Byron fell silent before rocking his hips gently from side to side, preparing for Lucifer's next push. Lucifer stroked the stretched edges of Byron's asshole gently, the skin angry and red but surprisingly intact, and spread a little more lube up his shaft. He slid his hand down over Byron's ass cheek.

"That's good. Now a bit more," he murmured. He felt Byron's body gradually relax, and he shook his head in wonder. Slowly, Lucifer pushed his cock in further, pausing again when Byron's body began to shudder between his hands, his low moan of pain rising to a strangled yell. Lucifer huffed out a few breaths and waited until Byron was quiet before shoving his cock the rest of the way in. This time the scream was almost piercing, and Lucifer stayed still for a few seconds, letting him get used to his girth. Byron's hole throbbed hard around his shaft, but he did nothing more than let out a small grunt when Lucifer pulled back slightly to force his cock in again.

"Wow," Lucifer murmured, with a soft laugh. Byron's response was another pained grunt as Lucifer's cock opened him up again, but it was quieter than the last. "Colour me impressed."

Lucifer fucked him deep for a few unhurried strokes before he leaned forward to sink his teeth into the back of Byron's shoulder— hard enough to hurt, but not enough to tear. When he got a sharp yelp in response, he closed his eyes and wrapped an arm around Byron's torso, plunging his cock faster, consumed by the slick, squeezing heat that enveloped him. The man beneath him had gone silent, only breathing heavily in time with his thrusts—Byron was neither pushing back into Lucifer or pulling away, simply remaining in place while the Devil used his body to bring himself to climax. When Lucifer did start to cum, he tasted blood as Byron's flesh finally ripped between his teeth—the resulting agonized cry caused Byron's ass to clench down harder on Lucifer's pistoning cock. Lucifer growled as he forced his load, spurt by thick spurt, into Byron's body before he finally came to a stop and lay panting atop him.

Groaning softly, he pulled his cock out and flopped onto his back beside Byron. There was only silence for a few breaths while Lucifer rubbed his face, buzzing from head to toe as he lay there recovering. When Byron hadn't yet moved, Lucifer frowned and looked over—on the floor beneath the trembling man was a puddle of bloodied cum, and more dripped slowly out of him. With a subtle gesture, Lucifer quickly cleaned up the mess and healed Byron.

With a sigh of relief, Byron collapsed onto his stomach on the cold floor and lay there motionless with his eyes closed.

A thoughtful expression on his face, Lucifer got to his feet, turned Byron over and gathered him up gently in his arms. Byron blinked up at him slowly, seeming dazed as Lucifer carried him into the other room and threw him down on the soft bed before lying down next to him.

"Thanks," Lucifer said gruffly. Sense came back gradually into Byron's eyes, and he nodded weakly.

"Don't mention it," came the response. It was followed by a quiet chuckle. "You didn't return my penis to me."

Lucifer yawned and scrubbed at his face. "I'll return it to you after I get a little shut-eye," he said, and then grinned. "I don't trust you with it." He was joking, of course. Nothing could happen to him. However, Byron just gave a tiny head nod and closed his eyes as if resigned to wait.

Staring at Byron's profile, Lucifer wondered again why it was that the man didn't fear him. Did it have something to do with Michael?

"Who is Michael, Byron?" he asked.

Byron turned his head and a furrow appeared between his blond brows.

"You keep bringing up that name. Michael who? Why is it so important?"

"It's just… odd. I'm being forced to wear his likeness for some reason, yet you don't even seem to recall him."

"You mentioned he was a victim of mine before. I swear I have no recollection of killing anyone named Michael." However, there was a tiny shred of doubt in Byron's expression.

"I have all of your records. The little girl you killed when you were nine. The homeless men when you were twelve and thirteen. Then the record after that simply says 'Michael.' No date. No family name. Then nothing until Gloria when you were twenty-two. Then one or two murders a year, mostly young men, until I came for you." He frowned. "You're telling me that I don't look familiar to you at all?"

Byron searched his face for a moment, but shook his head.

"You even mention Michael in at least one record."

"Where? Can I see these records you're referring to?"

Lucifer called forth Saeed's account and handed it over to Byron who immediately sat up on the bed and began flipping through the folder. After a moment, he looked up from the pages with a strange expression on his face.

"These are written in prose," he said.

"Yeah. So?" Lucifer stretched out, joints crackling, and yawned again. Though he had no need of sleep, he liked doing it. Especially after a really good orgasm. "My stenographer is an aspiring author. Besides, it makes it more interesting to read. Do you have any idea how dull these things are otherwise?"

Byron frowned down at the report, and his eyes flicked over the words until he found the reference to Michael. Lucifer folded his hands behind his head and watched.

"I don't know what to say," Byron said, slowly shaking his head. "I don't remember it."

Lucifer shut his eyes.

"I don't know what to tell you," he replied. "It's right there, plain as day."

Byron didn't say anything further, but Lucifer fell asleep to the sound of pages rustling as the serial killer read over his words again.

CONFUSED, BYRON FINALLY CLOSED THE FOLDER AND SAT thinking. He had so many questions but no one to answer them. He looked over at the Devil and had to smile. Lucifer's brow was smooth, and his lips were slightly parted as he dozed. In the dying rays of the afternoon sun, his skin was painted tawny, and as he breathed slow and deep, the striped shadows of the windowpane played over his chest. In his sleep, Lucifer was utterly charming in his seeming innocence. It was odd to think that Satan, Father of Lies, had such a young spirit. It wasn't just his appearance that gave Byron that impression. Even as a monstrous, horned devil—assuming that was his natural guise—it would be hard to mistake the sort of juvenile posturing one normally saw in teenagers.

Byron reached out and pushed a stray lock of dark hair out of Lucifer's face. Lucifer's nose twitched, and he sighed in response but didn't wake up. Yes, a rebellious teenager who never grew up.

Couldn't grow up? Byron wondered. And the weariness in his eyes, the shirking of his duties to hide among humans, the taste for torture lost… Lucifer was being punished by being forced to stay as he was. He had been given Byron as a special assignment, made to handle him personally… Yet no one had stopped their escape. And then there was his face—the handsome, bearded face of a young man that tugged at Byron's memories like chronic déjà vu, engendering vaguely tender and protective feelings towards him.

It was all very odd. As if everything had worked towards bringing them closer together. Even the hallucinated ghost of Gloria had helped to bring Lucifer and himself right to this point in time…

Byron looked up at Gloria. The tall woman stood leaning against the doorframe, her arms crossed and a rueful smile curving her full lips.

"I know who you are," said Byron.

"Oh?" asked Gloria. Her shapely brows rose a notch and she tilted her head at him. "And when did you figure that out?"

"Just now."

"Ah. Clever you." She walked towards him, her Louboutins clicking loudly on the wood floor, and settled into the plush gold and cream armchair near the bed. She folded one long, shapely leg over the other and smoothed down her slate-grey skirt. Her dark eyes narrowed a tiny bit in amusement as she appraised him.

Byron thought about the curious lightness that had followed his first brutal coupling with Lucifer and how Lucifer had been astonished by his youthful appearance. He guessed that without the face of Michael to hide his true form, the Devil would have been surprised to see himself looking much older. Things were starting to make a little more sense.

"Does he know what's happening to him?" he asked in a low voice.

Gloria picked something off her knee and let it fall from her red lacquered nails to the floor beside her. She shook her head.

"No. He knows that something is wrong, but he doesn't recognize what that is. It's been happening gradually, over hundreds of years," she replied in her husky voice. "Now it's up to you to finish the job… but one last thing is required."

Byron nodded.

"What is it that you need me to do?" he asked.

Gloria leaned forward in her chair, her smile dimpling her cheeks.

"I need you to remember."

LUCIFER THOUGHT HE HEARD VOICES, BUT WHEN HE OPENED his eyes, he saw only Byron on the bed next to him—though the room was dark, he could see his face clearly. Looking barely into his twenties, his skin had the glow of youth, and when he smiled, Lucifer found himself smiling back involuntarily.

"I know you," said Byron, an almost reverent note in his tone. "I *do* know you."

"What are you going on about?" Lucifer sat up and rubbed sleep from his eyes.

"It's the beard that threw me off," replied Byron, pointing. "See, Michael didn't have a beard. He was so young… We both were. Michael was just over fifteen when I killed him." His brows pinched together and his gaze became unfocused.

Impatient, Lucifer nodded, urging him on.

"Go on. What does it mean? Who was Michael?"

"He was my friend." Byron looked at Lucifer, a strange gleam in his eye. Then, when he began to speak again, Lucifer was stunned to discover himself remembering what had happened, as if he was there that far-off day.

As if he really *was* Michael.

MICHAEL ASHUR NASSAR
– 1962–1977

At the sound of something hitting the floor, Michael looked up from his textbook. Standing in the open doorway was the blondest and skinniest kid he'd ever seen. With the light of the hall shining brightly behind him, he reminded Michael of a dandelion gone to fluff. He was about to tell the kid to buzz off when he saw the big brown suitcase on the floor in front of him.

No fucking way. It was a third of the way through the semester —he'd thought for sure he'd remain solo in his room for the rest of the year.

"You in the right place?" he asked the kid. The blond boy just stared at him for a moment, his eyes pale and slightly watery looking, before he peered down at the crumpled paper clutched in his hand.

"Room seven in wing E," he read out loud. He glanced up at Michael. "This is E, right?"

"Great. Just fucking great," muttered Michael. He put the biology textbook facedown on his bed and got to his feet. "This is totally bogus. Lemme see that." He held out his hand, and the kid handed over the sheet, shifting his backpack awkwardly on his bony shoulder. Sure enough, right beneath all the admittance stuff was the room number. The red scribble beside it was barely legible, but Michael recognized the initials straight off.

"Bill Gorsky, that fucking *geek*," he said in disgust. "Who the hell does he think he is?" After the last time Michael had been caught smoking, Gorsky had said he'd keep a closer eye on him. "Are you here to narc on me?"

"I beg your pardon?" Blondie softened his *R*'s, like he had a touch of an accent. Michael looked again at the sheet.

"B. Danielsen? What is that, Swedish?"

"My family is originally from Norway," replied the boy. "But I'm third generation American." Another shift of the backpack. It looked too heavy for the kid to lift. "I've been mainly educated in England," he added. "This is my first time in an American boarding school." Blondie looked around the room and frowned at the clutter before continuing. "I haven't a clue what 'narcing' is, but I can assure you that I have no intention of doing it on you… or to you."

Michael curled his lip up in amusement.

"You know who you remind me of? That droid from *Star Wars*. C-3PO."

"I'm sorry?"

Nodding towards the big movie poster over his bed, Michael frowned at the look of incomprehension on the kid's face.

"What? You haven't seen it?"

Blondie shook his head.

Great. A total square. Michael sighed and reached out to take the bulky backpack from the kid's shoulder. The boy slumped in relief.

"Ok. I'm going to lay the skinny out for you, Danielsen," said Michael, dropping the pack down on the bed across the room. He set about picking up the lacrosse gear and stacks of comic books he'd been keeping on the spare bed. "You don't seem like a bad kid. But this is my crib. I was here first, so what I say *goes*. Dig?"

Michael was a little startled when he looked up at the boy and saw a strange, cold expression on his face. It passed in an instant, replaced by a wide, friendly smile.

"I'll try to stay out of your way," said the kid, holding his hand out. "It's Byron actually."

With a smirk, Michael stared down at Byron's hand for a second, wondering if he was for real. Then, with a shrug, he took it and shook hands with his new roommate.

"Michael," he said. "My friends call me Mike, but let's not get too friendly just yet. Maybe there's been a mix-up and you're meant to be in another room. And," he added, dropping the kid's hand. "Don't I ever hear you call me 'Mikey.'"

"I wouldn't dream of it," replied Byron with a little head tilt.

"Then we should get along just fine," Michael said and resumed moving his things from Byron's side of the room.

TRUE TO HIS WORD, BYRON STAYED OUT OF MICHAEL'S WAY. In fact, they barely saw each other at all except for in the evenings before lights-out. Michael's early-morning practices had him out of the room before Byron awoke; between classes and after lunch and supper, Byron was nowhere to be seen; and Friday nights, Michael's father sent a driver to pick him up so he could stay at home for the weekend. Michael had no idea if Byron went home. His side of the room was always neat and tidy, with no sign of his coming or going —so when Michael found Byron lying in bed one afternoon when he came looking for his chemistry textbook, he immediately knew something was wrong.

Michael frowned at the still figure huddled under the covers as he fished around under his own bed for the book. When his fingers came into contact with the corner of it, he pulled it out, but instead of leaving right away, he sat down on his mattress and stared at the back of Byron's head.

"You sick?" he asked finally. He waited in silence, wondering if he'd been heard. After a moment, Byron's shoulder moved under the scratchy navy-blue wool blanket.

"No," was the quiet reply. There was something in the way Byron moved again that struck Michael as odd. It was like he was shaking. He leaned forward.

"So… just getting some more shut-eye?" he said.

"Yes. Leave me alone."

Considering that Byron had been nothing but polite so far, his response was downright strange. Michael got to his feet and leaning over the boy in the bed, pulled the blanket back. The first thing that Michael noticed was the blood on the pillow. One step behind that was the smell of piss that assailed his nose.

"What the… ?"

Byron slowly turned his head to look at Michael. One of his eyes was swollen shut, and blood was smeared across his cheek, leaking slowly from a big, bruised cut. The other eye was wide, the pale-blue iris almost swallowed by his pupil. He let out a shuddering breath between lips gone bloodless, but his expression was defiant rather than scared.

"Who did this to you?" asked Michael quietly.

Byron's brows dipped a little, and he went back to resting his cheek on the pillow. Michael then noticed he was holding his arm to his chest—his wrist seemed swollen. When Bryon didn't reply, Michael reached out, but Byron just flinched.

"Don't touch me!"

Intrigued, but feeling some amount of pity for the skinny blond kid, Michael sat down beside him.

"Is it broken?" he asked quietly.

After a few seconds, Byron replied in a weak voice.

"I… I think so."

"If you let me take a look at it, maybe I can tell. I've taken both the first aid classes, you know."

Byron's eyes closed, and the corners of his mouth turned down, but he eventually turned onto his back slowly and let Michael take a look at his wrist.

"Yeah, I'd bet money that's broken," Michael said, gently moving it; Byron let out a hiss of pain. "So you're not gonna tell me who beat you up?"

"Who says someone beat me up?" asked Byron. To Michael's amazement, Byron gave him a crooked, devilish grin. "Perhaps I was the one beating someone up, and they fought back."

"Uh-huh." Michael smirked, looking pointedly at Byron's skinny arms. "You're a regular Bruce Banner."

"Who?"

"You're such a goddamn rube," replied Michael with a laugh. "Looks like I'm going to have to educate you."

"If you insist." Byron's face was pale from pain, but he looked amused.

"Ok, c'mon. Let's get you to the nurse."

JIMMY, THE HEAD BOY FOR THEIR FLOOR, POKED HIS HEAD around the door.

"It's lights-*out*," he said in a peeved voice. "Don't make me report you again, Nassar." The red pimples on his face stood out against his pale skin as he glared at Michael and Byron.

"Ok! We *got* it. Chill out, man. Seriously," said Michael. Jimmy stayed a moment longer, his ginger brows quivering with self-importance before slamming the door shut. "God, what a fucking spaz."

Michael leaned over and clicked off his lamp. Byron reached out for the one on the little bedside table beside him and let out a gasp of pain. With a sigh, Michael swung his legs over the side of the bed and crossed the room to give Byron a hand. Byron's wrist was broken in three places and was held together by pins—the worst thing was that the poor kid had the dumb luck of being resistant to painkillers. Michael couldn't imagine what that was like.

He pushed the little toggle switch and the room went dark. Next to him on the bed, Byron sighed.

"Thank you, Mike," he said. "I hate feeling so useless."

"Hey, that's what I'm here for, right?" He turned to go back to his bed, but when he hesitated, Byron touched him lightly on the arm, and he smiled.

"You're tired?" asked Byron.

"No," confessed Michael. The last few nights they had stayed up late talking about all sorts of things. Despite being pretty ignorant about movies and comic books, Byron actually was a pretty smart dude. Like Michael, he was planning on becoming a surgeon one day, and they shared notes on what they thought it would be like, cutting into people and all that.

Byron shifted slightly on the narrow mattress, making room, and Michael sat down, careful not to bump Byron's arm.

"Jimmy called you 'Nassar.' Is that your family name?" asked Byron's disembodied voice. It would take a few minutes before Michael's eyes would adjust to the dark.

"Yeah. Michael Ashur Nassar."

There was a moment of silence, and Michael wished he could see Byron's face.

"Oh. I don't know why, but I assumed you were of Spanish descent. So, you're an Arab?"

"I'm as much of an Arab as you're a Norwegian."

"Oh."

"My family's Assyrian."

"As in the ones from Mesopotamia?"

"Yeah. Descendants, you know?" Michael could just make out Byron's head on the pillow. "I do speak a little Arabic though," he confessed.

"Can you teach me?"

Michael liked Byron's cultured accent. The way it softened his words made him sound earnest, and with the lights off, he couldn't see the strange, sort of cold look that came over Byron's face sometimes.

"Sure," he replied.

The silence got a bit heavy as it stretched on, and Michael's heart started beating faster. He'd thought of something during biology class when he and his lab partner had been sniggering over the pictures of male anatomy. He couldn't get it out of his head.

"Hey, do you mind if I lie down here?" Michael asked, hoping that his voice didn't betray his nervousness. After a moment, Byron shifted again, moving closer to the wall.

"Be my guest."

Michael stretched out on the bed and put his head on the pillow. He could smell Byron's shampoo on it. However, when he adjusted his limbs to fit better on the narrow space, he managed to bump Byron's arm—Byron let out a pained grunt and then panted a few breaths. Awkwardly, Michael reached out to pat his shoulder.

"Sorry, dude. Sorry," he whispered. "Man, I still don't understand why you're protecting the guy who did this to you. What do you get out of it?"

Byron had told the nurse that he had fallen down the stairs, but Michael didn't believe it for a second.

"I told you I was the attacker," murmured Byron. "Not the other way around. I was injured when he fought back."

Michael rolled his eyes. It was an even worse lie than the stairs. Byron was a weird guy, but if he was going to pretend someone didn't beat the shit out of him, so be it.

"Next time you attack someone, I'd make sure you're carrying a syringe of something so you can drug 'em good so they can't fight back," he said, playing along.

"I'll remember that." It sounded like Byron was smiling.

Again it grew quiet, and Michael lay there listening to the blood whooshing in his ears like the sound of the surf, only ten times faster, trying to broach the subject that kept creeping back into his thoughts. He was getting a nervous boner just thinking about it. Finally, he closed his eyes and just went for it.

"You know, like, it's gotta totally suck that you broke the wrist on your jerking hand…" He tried to make it sound nonchalant.

"My jerking hand?" Byron, forever the rube.

"You know…" Michael gestured in the air, thumb and forefingers together, pretending to jerk a giant ghost cock above them in the gloom. For a second, he thought Byron couldn't see, but then he heard an awkward *hm*—it took a few beats before Byron replied in a strange, hoarse voice.

"I don't do that."

"Don't do what? Spank your monkey?" Michael asked, incredulous.

"Yes."

"What, like, *never*?"

"No."

"*Why*?"

"My mother once told me that if I did, I was going to Hell."

"That has got to be the stupidest thing I've ever heard. You can't tell me that you actually believe that!" He tried to imagine what that would be like, never having any kind of release. Sometimes when he had to go a day without doing it, it felt like his nuts were burning. "That's crazy."

"No, I don't actually *believe* her. It's just that I'm not sure about how… Well… I don't really know…" Byron sounded embarrassed.

"You don't know *how*?" asked Michael, rolling over onto his side. Byron lay there quietly in the dark, just the tiny, reflected glitter of light in his eyes to show he was looking at Michael. He shook his head.

They lay there in the dark, staring at each other until Michael finally just blurted it out.

"I can show you."

"Oh." Byron seemed to mull it over in silence while Michael almost squirmed in anticipation, hoping that he hadn't come off as a total pervert. He told himself that if Byron said no, he'd go back to his bed, and they would never talk about it again. However, from the other side of the bed came a quiet sigh.

"I think I'd like that."

His hard-on throbbing in his pj bottoms, Michael lay there stunned for a moment, almost too shy to move all of a sudden. Then he cleared his throat, and trying to sound like he'd done this before, he reached over and touched Byron's chest softly.

"Well, since your wrist's busted… I'll just quickly show you, like, the basics," he said. "With my hand."

"Ok." Byron's breathing had gotten a little faster, and Michael felt the blood hot in his face.

"Do you want to, um, pull the blanket down?"

Quickly, Byron pushed the wool cover down to his thighs. Michael could just make out the bulge tenting the material of his pj's. Licking his lips, he moved his hand down. And then further down. It sounded like Byron was holding his breath. Finally, his palm touched a hot, hard something through the thin fabric. It moved against his hand, and Byron let out a huff of breath.

"Do you want me to do it like this? You know? Through your pants?" He swallowed, trying not to sound like an amateur. "Or… under?" Again, there was a long pause before Byron replied.

"Under."

Hand shaking a tiny bit, Michael fumbled with the cord but managed to drag down the waist of Byron's pj bottoms, Byron rocking his hips slightly to dislodge the material beneath him.

Then he groped around in the dark and found *it*.

Byron's dick was longer than his, but skinnier, and Michael's heart raced so fast he thought he would pass out.

Holy shit, you've got your hand on another guy's dick! Eyes closed and jaw clenched, Michael had to take a few deep breaths to calm himself before starting his "lesson." He began to jerk off Byron's cock like he did his own. He'd intended on narrating his lesson like they did on TV when demonstrated something but found he couldn't speak.

After only a few strokes, Byron let out a quiet *oh* and Michael felt something warm run down over his fingers. With a nearly silent moan, Michael yanked down the front of his pants and frantically jerked himself off using Byron's cum. When he'd exploded all over his belly, he lay there panting. Then, before it got too weird, he slipped off Byron's bed and grabbed a few tissues out of the box before tossing it in Byron's direction. He wiped himself down and heard his roommate fumbling in the dark. Feeling a little stunned and awkward in the aftermath, Michael lay down on his bed.

"So. That's how you do it," he said to the ceiling after a few minutes.

"I see," came the reply.

Michael frowned, not knowing what to make of Byron's unenthusiastic response. The guy was so weird sometimes, a real cold fish.

"Can you show me again sometime?" asked Byron softly.

Face creased in a huge smile, Michael looked over in the direction of the other bed.

"For sure, buddy. Anytime."

"Thank you, Mike."

"Uh-huh," Michael replied. It wasn't long before he heard Byron's breathing even out into the rhythm of sleep, and he turned on his side, staring at the barely visible shape across the room and wondering if Byron's cum tasted anything like his own.

Byron's "lessons" continued daily, almost always after lights-out, but occasionally, they made plans to meet at the room over lunch. Michael became more confident and curious, trying out different ways of getting Byron off, and both of them looked so forward to their little trysts that it spilled into their public behaviour. Though Byron was a year behind Michael, Michael often went to meet Byron after his classes so they could walk down the big echoing hall together. Then, when one of the phys ed teachers suddenly up and quit halfway through the last semester, two classes had to be combined, and Michael and Byron found themselves sharing a course.

One day, during last period, Michael sat on Byron's feet, watching him do sit-ups. Every time Byron came up he smiled, and Michael smiled back. He thought that Byron was really learning to chill out—he wasn't half as frigid and weird as he'd been when they first met. Michael really liked him. Like, a lot. When Byron's cast had come off, he'd begun to reciprocate during their little sessions together, claiming that it was really good for him to be building up strength in his wrist. Afterwards they would snuggle a bit before parting ways, even though the lack of door locks made discovery a constant threat. While it was really awesome to have another guy jerk him off, Michael found himself craving those quiet moments together when they were acting like boyfriends nearly as much.

"C'mon, you skinny little geek!" he teased when Byron began to slow. "You got at least four more in you."

"Yeah, I'm sure what he'd like is something else 'in him,' " said a voice behind him. "If you know what I mean."

Michael turned his head and saw Chester with his little gang of stooges.

"Take a hike," said Michael and turned back to Byron. Byron lay on the ground, his hands behind his head, with a strange expression on his face.

"I hear you've been giving it to him goooood. Or… Is it the other way 'round?"

Michael clenched his jaw, his heart beating fast, and rose to his feet. Though he was starkly terrified over the discovery, he stepped up close to Chester, enough that he could see the blackheads on his cheeks, and said in a low voice:

"You're tripping, man. I've got no idea what the hell you're talking about, so beat it before I beat *you*."

"Oh look, guys, I made the little faggot mad," crooned Chester with an exaggerated pout. The meatheads behind him sniggered. "Tell me, Nassar, are you the girl when you fuck? Do you let him stick it to you?"

"Fuck you," growled Michael. Chester was a bully, but he'd never had any cause to bother him before. In fact, they'd often been partners in phys ed before the younger class joined them. Michael knew there was no way they had been spotted doing anything, but he was kicking himself for being so *obvious* around Byron. That's all it took really, a smile too many, maybe sitting too close, for rumours to fly.

"No fuck *you*," replied Chester, pushing his chest out. "I'm glad I found out now before you had a chance to grab my ass, you *queer*. Wait until I tell my dad. You'll get expelled so fast…"

Michael's heart stopped. This went further than a beating. Chester's dad was on the parent council and donated vast amounts to the school every year… and of course he'd believe his cretin of a son. Terrified of what would happen if he were expelled for being a homosexual and of what his own father would do to him because of it, he put his hands up.

"Whoa! Take a chill pill, man," he said. "No cause for that. I just think you're mistaken, *friend*."

"I'm not your friend, cocksucker. You and your little girlfriend are sick fuckos. My dad says that all faggots need lobotom—"

A surprised hiccup of pain burst out of Chester when Byron tackled him to the ground, knocking the breath out of him. With a growl, the slight blond boy grabbed Chester by the ears and began to dash his head hard against the packed sod as the bully struggled to choke in some air.

It was as if everything went real slow for a moment, everyone too startled to react. Then Chester's cronies sprang into action when their leader let out a yell, his hands grappling at Byron, trying to dislodge him. Michael took a punch to the face when he jumped into the fight, but Byron, punching and wind milling his arms like a madman, managed to get loose. Michael pushed one of the boys to the ground and then heard the shrill sound of the whistle. Everyone stopped in their tracks as Coach Harvey jogged towards him. However, Michael saw Byron smile at Chester who was still lying in the grass before he kicked him as hard as he could in the jaw.

Though only the surrounding group heard the crack, everyone on the field heard the resulting scream.

UNLIKE MICHAEL, BYRON HADN'T SUFFERED A SINGLE INJURY during the fight, and he sat on the bed, hands clasped in his lap, staring at Michael who was gingerly prodding at the bruise on his cheek.

"You know you're going to get expelled," said Michael.

Byron shrugged as if he didn't care one way or another.

"And me too."

"No. You won't. I'll make sure of it," said Byron. "Chester's father isn't the only one who likes to pad the school's coffers."

"But my dad's going to literally kill me when he finds out what the fight is about."

Byron's expression went cold and dark for a second, and Michael felt the tiniest sliver of fear. Or, maybe it was awe. Byron had fought like a maniac and didn't seem the least bit concerned about it. For the first time, Michael wondered if whether Byron hadn't been lying about starting the fight that had landed him a broken wrist.

"You know what? It'll be fine," Michael said, feeling compelled to downplay what his father's reaction would be. "He won't believe it anyway."

"That you're a homosexual?"

Michael cringed at the word. "Shuddup."

"Well, aren't you?" Byron tilted his head, his pale-blue eyes curious.

"If I am, so are you," hissed Michael, his anger fuelled by fear of being overheard.

"I… don't think so."

"What the hell do you think it means when two guys do *things* together? Huh? Don't be such a fucking rube, Byron. You're a faggot just like me."

"I don't like that word. Don't use that word."

"Faggot!" Michael knew he was just reacting to being so scared… for his hide when his old man got through with him, but even more over the thought of losing what he had with Byron. He felt a panicky hollow in his belly at the thought of being separated from him.

Byron rose from the bed, and without a word, he picked up one of the wooden desk chairs and wedged it on its back into the space between Michael's bed and the door. The top of the chair rested against the bottom of the door, while one of the back legs was braced on the corner of the bedpost. If anyone tried to open the door, it would stay jammed shut. Michael raised his eyebrows.

"Why didn't we do that before?"

Byron ignored his question and got onto the bed with him.

"Ok. If I'm gay, then there's something I would like to try."

Michael blinked.

"What *now*? They're going to come for us as soon as they reach a decision."

"I know. But it won't be for a little while yet. I just want to try jerking you off with my mouth."

"*What?*" Michael was a bit taken aback by just how clinical Byron could make things sound. However, his words gave his dick a rise anyway. He lay down when Byron pushed him back gently, and he helped him get his trousers down around his thighs. His cock lay half-asleep in the crinkly black thatch, but when Byron reached for it, it moved a little. Byron leaned forward and kissed the shaft with dry lips.

"Wow, you're serious?" Michael said, his voice hoarse.

"I am."

"Why now? I… I mean, don't, ohhh"—Michael grabbed hold of the back of Byron's head when the boy's tongue touched him— "don't stop. It's just… oh *fuck*. Yeah… *wow*."

Byron licked his lips and smiled at Michael when he paused in his slow savouring of Michael's cock.

"I… *like* you, Mike," Byron said, squeezing his shaft gently. The air cooled the saliva on the head of Michael's cock, and he almost whimpered, wanting more of Byron's mouth, but Byron continued. "I know this probably means the end of whatever this is between us. Either I'm expelled, or both of us, and I very much doubt we'll see each other again. I just wanted to leave you with something nice to remember me by."

"Yeah. Something nice," Michael whispered and then arched his head back on the pillow when Byron's mouth enveloped him again. "And it's called a blowjob, you know." He began shifting his hips in the same rhythm. His first blowjob. It was wonderful, and almost enough for him to ignore what Byron had just said about never seeing each other again.

He let out a groan when he was on the cusp, and then suddenly worried he wasn't supposed to cum in Byron's mouth, he tried to push him away, but there it was, hot and intense, spurting onto Byron's soft tongue, and he just shuddered with his release.

Byron sat up a moment later, swallowing everything, and it made Michael laugh to see his pensive expression over the taste of it.

"You didn't have to take my load, you know," he said, but he was really glad he had. There was something really hot about knowing that Byron had swallowed his cum.

"It was my pleasure," responded Byron, wiping his mouth with the back of his hand. "Now… I have something for you."

"Oh, man," said Michael, shaking his head. "Don't do this. You don't know that we'll never see each other again. You're making me real sad, dude." He said it jokingly, but he felt weirdly choked up about it. Like he would cry if he thought too much about it.

"It's ok… I want to give it to you anyway," said Byron with an affectionate smile. "But you have to close your eyes."

"Fine," said Michael, scrunching his nose. "But I have nothing for you."

"Close your eyes."

With a sigh, Michael closed his eyes, his heart heavy but curious as to what Byron had gotten him. Maybe it was the AT-AT model that he'd been going on—

Something crashed into his face. Pain. Blinding pain. Then warmth.

Then nothing.

THE END

Lucifer startled out of the vision, and he choked on his breath. He'd been dead for a moment, and it was surprisingly terrifying. He felt utterly confused. Sad, angry, completely shocked… betrayed.

"You *killed* him?" he managed, staring wide-eyed at Byron who sat watching him impassively. The blond man now looked only a few years older than he had in the vision.

"I did."

"*Why?*" Lucifer was reeling. "You said you *liked* him."

"Yes. I very much liked Michael. I think I liked him more than I've ever liked any human being my whole life," replied Byron, lifting one shoulder.

"But you killed him anyway."

Byron nodded. There wasn't a shred of emotion on his face.

"I clubbed him to death with his lacrosse trophy," he answered. "Then I freed the door, tore my shirt, and when they found me, I was curled up in a ball, acting terrified."

Lucifer shook his head slowly from side to side.

"But *why?*"

"I said that he had tried to touch me and that while defending myself, he had gotten rough. I killed him out of self-defence."

"And they believed you." Lucifer was stunned. There was a sick feeling in the pit of his stomach. Part of him was still Michael. Still the boy who thought Byron was something other than he was. He closed his eyes and swallowed thickly. He'd *trusted* Byron. Was very nearly in love with him.

"And they believed me," agreed Byron. Lucifer opened his eyes when his arm was touched. "Truly, I wouldn't have killed him, but I didn't have a choice. That school was my last chance. I'd been kicked out of every other decent boarding school."

"You killed me—*him* because of *that*?"

"Yes."

"You don't have a single shred of remorse, do you?"

"None."

Lucifer felt like screaming.

"Then, *why*? Why the hell was I forced to wear Michael's face if it wasn't to trigger some kind of *feeling* out of you? Why the secrecy over his death? What was all of this for? Why?" He sounded slightly hysterical. "Why did the council put me through all of this if it wasn't going to amount to *shit*?"

"Easy," said Byron with a smile. "It was for *you*."

"What? How?"

"Because they needed you to like me."

"Like you? Why?" Lucifer was so confused. He didn't want to like Byron… but he *did*, and it wasn't entirely the fault of the vision.

"Because then *this*"—Lucifer's butcher knife appeared in Byron's hand, and he slammed it to the hilt into Lucifer's chest—"would become possible."

STUNNED, LUCIFER LET OUT A HARSH BREATH AND SAT THERE, staring at the handle of the knife sticking out of his chest. Byron shouldn't have been able to stab him—though with everything Byron had managed so far, it wasn't as much of a surprise as it ought to be.

"How?" he gasped and keeled over sideways on the bed, his life energy draining into the air. The red mist swirled as Byron pulled Lucifer into his arms and held him gently, stroking his hair.

"The memories of Michael had been stolen from me years ago when my parents forced me into electroshock therapy," Byron said quietly, his touch soft. "However, enough remained behind that when I saw your face, *his* face, it drew me to you. *That's* why I would have let you live. That's why I trusted you. That's why your presence made me less afraid. I didn't recognize your face, but I instinctively *knew* it."

Lucifer grabbed at the handle of the knife weakly, but his hand passed right through.

"How?" He couldn't understand how Byron had made the vision happen, or how he had made the blade appear.

"Your maker came to see me earlier and explained things to me."

"My… maker?"

"Yes. Turns out that we've known each other for quite some time. One big, long job interview, I suppose," Byron said, running his fingers along the curve of Michael's jaw. Despite the fact that he felt like he was dying, the contact was soothing. "They took away your ability to read my mind once we were in Hell because you would have quickly uncovered the truth about Michael, locked away in my brain. The only reason you didn't at my house was because your maker was there, personally making sure you didn't. They needed me to trust you, so that you would, in turn, open up to me. They gave me back the memory of Michael, and I was able to give it to you."

"But for what?"

"To trigger the final seeds of Good in you that needed a little extra push. You liked me well enough, despite everything, but you needed to really *feel* it. And that's what Michael provided."

"But I'm not human!" whispered Lucifer. He felt like he was melting away into the air.

"No, you're not. But you've been around them long enough that you've been contaminated somewhat. That's where your apathy and discontent stemmed from. You've been gathering seeds for a long time that have no business being inside you."

"Huh." Lucifer closed his eyes. He could feel the Light drawing him in, and he felt both confused and hopeful.

"Yes," Byron said with a chuckle. "You're being called home. Your maker has decided that you deserve it. Consider it a promotion."

"Oh," mouthed Lucifer, falling away.

BYRON LOOKED AT THE LUMINOUS CREATURE THAT LAY IN HIS lap. Delicate features, shining skin covered in crystal scales, diaphanous wings that shimmered with every colour of the rainbow… Even the small, curved horns on Lucifer's forehead looked as if they were made of opal. With Michael's features peeled away, what was left behind was one of the most beautiful beings that Byron had ever seen. With a smile, Byron pulled out the blade, freeing Lucifer's form. It faded from sight.

"Good work," said Gloria.

Byron glanced up and nodded.

"Thank you," he replied and sent the blade back into the ether. "Am I free to make whatever changes I like to the system?"

"Of course," said Gloria. "It'll be nice to have a change after so long."

"Good, because I have numerous ideas that I think would speed things up."

"Excellent. Go to it." Gloria winked out.

Byron stood, the layers of reality that surrounded him shifting and bending with his movements. He felt the power in the pit of his stomach like a raging storm and was anxious to get to work. Lifting a hand, he smiled when he saw the red mist swirling around it.

BYRON FOLDED SPACE AND TOOK HIMSELF TO LUCIFER'S OLD office in Hell. He looked around at the mismatched furniture and the messy desk and wrinkled his nose. With a flick of his fingers, the room was filled with tasteful yet comfortable cream-coloured couches and a big antique mahogany and satinwood pedestal desk. He frowned when he saw something wrapped in plain brown paper suddenly appear on the green blotter in the centre of the desk. "Ombra Fedele Anch'io" began to play softly as he picked up the package.

He read the small tag attached to it:

Byron,

    Ditch the butcher's knife—that was my gig. I thought this would suit you better.

    Thanks and good luck, you fucking psycho.

— LUCE

Byron unwrapped the gift and held up the ivory-handled bone saw. He chuckled. Yes, it suited him much better. He hung it above the desk, smiled, and then left to address the teeming masses that awaited him below.

Other Books by Bey Deckard

Max, the Series

Max

Max, the Sequel

Baal's Heart Series

Caged: Love and Treachery on the High Seas

Sacrificed: Heart Beyond the Spires

Fated: Blood and Redemption

Careened: Winter Solstice in Madierus

F.I.S.T.S

Sarge

Murphy

F.I.S.T.S. Handbook For Individual Survival in Hostile Environments

The Actor's Circle

The Complications of T

The Last Nights of The Frangipani Hotel

The Stonewatchers

Kestrel's Talon

Standalone Books

Uncle Zach

Better the Devil You Know

Exposed

Beauty and His Beast

The Blacksmith's Apprentice

SHORT STORIES

Don't Touch Me (UnCommon Bodies Anthology)

Rakka Surprise (UnCommon Lands Anthology)

About the Author

Artist, Writer, Dog Lover

Bey Deckard is the author of a number of novels including the *Baal's Heart books, Max, Beauty and His Beast,* and *Better the Devil You Know.*

Bey lives in Montréal, Canada where he spends most of his time writing, doing graphic work, painting portraits, speaking French, cooking tasty vegetarian eats, or watching more movies than is good for him. If you're the curious type, www.beydeckard.com is where you'll find art and free stories by Bey as well as information on his published works.

bey.deckard@gmail.com
Look for Deckard's Diablerie on Facebook

facebook.com/authorbeydeckard

x.com/BeyDeckard

instagram.com/beydeckard

goodreads.com/beydeckard

bookbub.com/authors/bey-deckard

pettingzoo.co/@Beybey

threads.net/@beydeckard